Metaphorosis

March 2023

Beautifully made speculative fiction

Also from Metaphorosis

Metaphorosis Magazine

Metaphorosis: Best of 20xx
Metaphorosis 20xx: The Complete Stories
annual issues, from 2016

Monthly issues

Plant Based Press

Best Vegan Science Fiction & Fantasy
annual issues, 2016-2020

from B. Morris Allen:
Chambers of the Heart: speculative stories
Susurrus
Allenthology: Volume I
Tocsin: and other stories
Start with Stones: collected stories
Metaphorosis: a collection of stories

Verdage

Reading 5X5 x3: Changes
Reading 5X5 x2: Duets
Score – an SFF symphony
Reading 5X5: Readers' Edition
Reading 5X5: Writers' Edition

Vestige

The Nocturnals, by Mariah Montoya

Metaphorosis

March 2023

edited by
B. Morris Allen

ISSN: 2573-136X (online)
ISBN: 978-1-64076-253-4 (e-book)
ISBN: 978-1-64076-254-1 (paperback)

Metaphorosis
a magazine of speculative fiction
from
Metaphorosis Publishing

Neskowin

March 2023

All the Daughters Sing

Jan Priddy

Light pours straight down through the leaves, hot like midsummer, and the duff underfoot feels quite light and dry. Yes, it must be July. The moon has gone bright and dark and bright again without more than a mist falling. Salmonberries are ripening.

I move along the narrow path, using a staff of carved cedar wood because I tire easily, and my feet are unsteady on the path. Sometimes my attention wanders. I mean to be quick, sneaking away for this last walk alone. Daughters will come soon enough and spoil my solitude.

My goal is the large mossed-over stone marking where my first daughter is buried. My firstborn, Alice. The trees are deciduous along this slope. Thin branches and spicy leaves rattle with the slightest breeze, but the air hardly stirs, passing in and out of my open mouth without a sound, blood-warm as if I walk through the world's breath.

I hold my breath and listen. No sound of Daughters behind me, though they will follow if they catch me wandering. They are light on their feet, careful even when it does not matter.

Being alone is the point of my walk, and there is no one looking to disagree. I only argue with myself. Daughters never argue. They listen. They are respectful of my opinions, my cautions and concerns. Yet, as I walk, I feel hemmed in and worried by something more, just out of sight. I should have told them where I was going and asked them to leave me be. They would have done that.

Waiting is an ache beneath my heart, the thudding sound of it, and desire for an ending.

Movement catches my attention just ahead and above, a fluttering like—very much like—something living. It stutters and drifts across the perfectly still air, down and down, like something alive, like a butterfly, and I have nearly forgotten what a butterfly was like after all this time. I track its movement along the downslope ahead of me, near Alice's grave. Wonder flutters from joy to loss. I reach above my head to catch it, fingers splayed and reaching, mouth open, attention gathered completely by the movement where there should be no movement.

As I reach to grasp the butterfly, just beyond the tips of my fingers, I step wrong and wound myself. I sit abruptly on the dry earth—the out-of-season leaf drops nearby—and pull my foot into my lap, where blood wells from my broken skin. Much has been broken. This hillside once had homes with windows and kitchens and families.

I squeeze the tough sole of my foot, remove a sliver of green glass the size of a fingernail. Glass, after all this time. Decades crept past.

Since I was born, people warned the world might end in a blaze or with a whimper. Climate and catastrophe were always the story. Death from disease or some newly recognized toxin. Is that how it happened? I do not care. Instead, I fear sometimes I will never die. I survived a century and more past my time.

The light splatters down between the trees, their pale leaves unspeaking in the stillness.

Too soon, Daughters will scent blood and come running quick as anything.

In the middle of the twenty-first century, no British swallow returned from South Africa. Terns, wheatears, and sheerwaters vanished from their migratory routes. Sandhill cranes failed to return to wetlands in Michigan where they had rested and nested for nine million years. By then, seagulls no longer trailed fishing fleets. Bird feeders, attracted only determined squirrels and chipmunks and rats. Small children playing in their own back yards carried festering bodies of songbirds to their horrified parents.

If anyone had predicted what happened, it would have been a worst case scenario. No one wanted to believe we would be helpless to fight it off.

I might have been among the first human beings to catch the new virus. Or perhaps it was a very old one. Or a bacterium. Or maybe several diseases that also killed birds and snakes and frogs and then mammals. There would be no one left to study and explain what killed them all—whatever it was that made me sick, but not dead. I will never know. I refuse to care how it happened. I will never know why or how or what will come later. For a long time I only focused on the now.

But when it started long ago, I lay under blankets, eyes closed, and shivered for what seemed an eternity. Hours? A day? I told my flatmate I needed to sleep and turned off my cell. At first, I assumed it was a cold coming on suddenly after work, then, later in the evening and the following days, some really bad influenza or another mutation of the coronavirus that would not let go. In bed, too weak to dress and go to work or even to call in sick, I messaged my boss and collapsed. My joints ached, skin wet with fever, but on a trip to the bathroom I tucked a thermometer into my ear and found my temperature had dropped to 95°. I staggered back to bed and to sleep. I was not yet afraid of dying. I was afraid of missing work, of not being prepared for the trade show presentation. I was afraid I would lose my job. I turned on my cell to message my boss again and scrolled through for news. Headlines declared that whole cities were getting sick and dying. I was afraid I would catch whatever those other people had. Despite being afraid I might die, I did not die. Instead, I felt better.

It was a Tuesday when I finally felt well enough to call into work, but service was down and I felt too wretched to care. My joints crackled when I sat up in bed. I could not hear my flatmates in the central kitchen or Carly slamming the door as she left early for work. Carly always slammed the front door. I could time my day by the slam and her stomping down the stairs.

I sniffed. What was that awful smell?

The stink was what finally drove me from bed and to the kitchen. No one there and I was sick, that was all. I drank a glass bottle of water, scrolled through screens that refused to open properly, opened blinds to check the street, but all was silent. There was power from the passive system I'd set up, and water ran from the tap when I washed my hands. But it was quiet. No traffic, no neighbor's dog barked, no one played music. I wiped my eyes unstuck as I stood at the window. The air outside seemed thicker, misty almost, and my ears rang with a hissing, stinging sound that gave way to absolute silence, the quiet like a presence waiting. I wanted to lie back down. By that Tuesday —if it was a Tuesday—life on Earth, most everything that moved, had ended. Whatever it was had killed everyone I knew and entire populations I never could have known, though I did not understand that at the time.

I held myself quite calm when telling Daughters this story, emotions carefully in check. I had not been calm in those early years alone. I cried and screamed and shook and shouted at the silence. I ran through empty streets in the dark and walked for days south to the Columbia River and found no one, saw nothing that mattered.

Herds of deer did not dash through downtown canyons of concrete. I did not track the days with marks scratched onto a wall. I did not make plans to walk across the continent or to rebuild. Climate change had already done its dirty deed, invaded shorelines, stolen entire low-lying neighborhoods and left winters damp but mild. The filthy air blew away and I breathed easier. I accepted all that. I cannot explain, but I knew everything was changed forever and I made no effort to change things back.

I do not tell the Daughters any of this.

Even in those first days, there was no doubt what was behind Carly's closed bedroom door. For a long time I huddled in my room, left only to drink bottled water, eat peas and broccoli thawing in the freezer, cold canned chili and the last banana, already gone soupy inside. It was crazy, but I thought everything would be all right if I remained calm, if I did not open Carley's door or try to call my mother. That horrible smell. Flies everywhere. Plastics breaking down faster than they should.

Odors of chlorine and vinegar overrode the rot. My stored food ran out, and I went out to the grocery store over on 45th and thought about theft. From whom? I tried the doors, banged on them, threw rocks from a garden, but could not break the glass. I found an ancient push mower in the storage room of my condo, carried it down to the corner, and tossed it through the front window of the local convenience store. By that time, I had gotten used to the stink, or it was fading—I hoped it was. Entire human bodies collapsed into puddles and stains sliding across sidewalks leaving huddles of chemical clothing even the insects did not eat. Packages of crackers and cookies were spoiled and nibbled, but glass containers and cans were fine. Sell-by dates meant nothing. Weeks or months passed; I was already losing track of time.

I went out under the stars and searched for the sound of something larger than a carpenter ant. I had not yet noticed I was not sleeping. I knew my friends were dead, my family, my job didn't matter. I did not have to complete my presentation on post-graphene batteries or defend the generation after that.

My watch quit working. My sport shoes smelled of vinegar and went flat. I thought I would have to give up running. The idea made me laugh and recognize how near I was to hysteria.

I made the list in my head: food, water, shelter. Family. Mom had called when her canaries died. I was already sick that day. My mother. I went to find her. Mom's house was collapsing and I could not breathe. I sat in the road and could not get back to what I knew or the people. Everyone was gone. I closed my eyes and waited for the days to end. For the nights to pass. By now, I knew I was not sleeping.

The moon had gone to full by then—I could see the moon when I went out, streets lit by stars that had once been obscured by artificial lights. I walked all the way into downtown, past wooden buildings that seemed already to tip and sag. Stains on the sidewalks all the way to the waterfront and up against the inside of glass doors to office buildings. No bodies, the stink fading away.

I broke into the REI downtown, found flint and steel, a small folding shovel with a metal handle. Even this building was not steady, would not last long. From this and other stores I gathered everything that might be useful and not rot and dragged it outside to the middle of streets where I hoped I could find it if I needed something later.

Anything in freezers or refrigerated cases was hopeless. Cardboard packaging was eaten through, plastic containers were corroded and discolored. Ants fell from the ceiling onto my head as I collected glass bottles of sun-dried tomatoes, olives, and sweet red peppers, cans of beans and tomatoes, fancy flavored salt packaged in glass.

I was very tired, but kept moving, seeking something familiar. I climbed back east through empty streets, broke into the Conservatory on Capital Hill. It had been my peaceful place, but now the plants in the center pavillion were dry and dead. Downtown again, I learned the trick to breaking tempered glass and smashed windows just to hear them fall. When my clothing fell apart, I broke locks on doors and found more. When I was hungry, I found whatever was nearest. I ate canned food shelved in the upper floors of downtown condominium kitchens, and built fires on their concrete floors to give light in the lengthening nights.

I closed my eyes, imagined sleep.

Some days, I cried and screamed and argued out loud with myself. On a long walk south, I raided small towns and tried to remember their names. Arms wrapped around my body, pacing the freeway and empty sidewalks that had begun to go cockeyed and too hot for bare feet. There was no one walking larger than a beetle. One sweltering summer day I came upon a river of black ants moving across the floor of an empty house, felt the crunch and moisture of their bodies under my naked heels, around and across my feet. Caught between fascination and fury, I stamped and stamped them, until, hysterical and sobbing, I had to run away from the squashed and swarming bodies. I closed my mouth on my remorse. The world was quieter, and I became quiet. There was nothing to see across the Columbia River, only another city falling down. I went north to home in Seattle. The word 'home' in my head made me laugh.

I thought about walking off the edge of a building or taking pills found in a pharmacy, or sleeping until the world ended. If only I could sleep. I leaned too close to fire though I was not cold, only alone and shivering. What threatened? No strangers. No dogs or wild animals drawn by flame. I remembered moths fluttering and dropping into campfires on the walk south, but there were no moths by the time I walked north again. Fewer flies. I walked for miles until I was too tired to walk further. I thought I would die.

When there were no longer shoes or clothing remaining from Before, I went naked and did not feel the cold even at night. I sat in shade in hot weather, found shelter from wind when the air cooled. I managed. I ate anything I could find or gather without craving any particular food. I was never sick. I remembered snow and books and family dinners. But it was never cold enough for frost and my books fell apart and all my family was dead.

I had been alone, entirely alone for years, when I realized I was pregnant.

One morning after bathing in the vast basin that I thought of as Lake Washington, I ran my hands across my stomach and felt the knot flutter below my belly button. My monthly periods had ceased long ago—how long? I should have been grateful; where would I find tampons? I was relieved, wasn't I? I could not recall precisely when my monthlies had become yearlies, only that my last period had been a month ago. I argued with myself about the bulge in my belly: a parasite? But soon my belly grew round and tight. It was a baby turning under my hand.

I could not be pregnant.

In late spring, just weeks after I understood my condition, contractions began.

I deliberately turned away from both reason and fear. It was a miscarriage. Of course it was. I was losing the baby, and though tears came and my hands shook and I panted, I told myself it was all for the best. I could not have a baby alone. I could not have a baby at all. There was only the tiny bulge in my belly, not the enormous belly holding a full term infant. I breathed steadily, sat in the shade of a dying maple tree, and counted between passes of pain that was not quite pain but something else. Ripples of heat in my body—an orgasm, pleasure, and I was startled, then howling, screaming in pleasure and shuddering in that long forgotten ecstasy—how could I have forgotten this?

It seemed to last a long time, this pulsing pleasure and pain. Then, hardly noticing I did, I pushed it out. A sliding, climactic birth throb, and a blueish, blood-streaked sack lay between my thighs, born in a series of overwhelming orgasmic pulses. I gasped and closed my eyes, then, remembering something I had not known, I bent to tear open the sack with my nails. The slick covering membrane was tough and I used my teeth. It stretched, tore, and the tiniest infant pushed its face out. I cleared the sack. The infant lay on the new grass, slick and wet and mewling like a puppy. Alive. Tiny. I thought the baby would surely die—the size of two fists stacked end to end, barely as long as my fingers spread wide—helpless and dark. But it was strong. The baby screamed, and I gathered it against my bare chest. It hunted for a breast. Latched. Milk came, and the infant girl suckled.

Miraculous and marvelous. Another ripple of pleasure—again that pulse I could not help connecting to sex—echoed as my baby nursed, my whole body hot and glowing. What a blessing to feel pleasure and to be of use! I wiped my daughter clean with grass. She did not die that day.

My daughter's eyes were nearly black rather than my hazel, darker than my grandmother's eyes were said to have been. The baby's skin, too, showed darker than mine, matching where mine was browned by the sun, but she had that rich color at birth. My beautiful Alice.

It was still spring when she slid out of my arms and stood. The child was not growing the way children were supposed to grow. Surely my nephew had been nearly a year before he stood unaided. I pushed the memory away.

Alice laughed, a burbling chuckle, ending in a squeal as she took a step away from me. She toddled toward a tuft of clover, stumbled on a stone and splashed the still water in a puddle.

I stood over the infant, steadying her shoulders between my hands.

"Okay, little one. Come along now," I said, meaning to guide her away from the murky water.

The child looked around, frowned, and said, "Okay."

My legs let me down onto the ground as if I'd fallen. I recognized then what I had refused to see before. I whispered to my already sturdy child, "Baby girl, little Alice, where did you come from?"

The tiny child looked up to my face and said, "Come from?"

It was all crazy, wonderful. I laughed and swung Alice onto my hip and then set her down, swung her up and over my head.

I laughed for the madness of it all—having a child, a child who stood in days, a child who did not resemble me at all. Like everything gone—the absence of dogs howling at the moon, no cats sleeping in sunshine, no birds, collapsing houses in the city—this child was something new and different.

But then, what was not? My mother had been fond of the expression, "So what else is new?" I watched my tiny daughter tumbling in the grass and whispered, not quite to myself, "Everything."

I released myself from control and ran and laughed with Alice.

Before the first leaves turned and fell, Alice kept pace with me all day. She helped gather filberts on the other side of the lake, trailing after wherever I went, talking and singing too. My voice had been near silent, but now we chattered all day. I sang her to sleep and closed my own eyes and imagined what we might do next. We moved closer to the city, I made her toys from scraps of wood and taught her songs recalled from childhood, and my little girl sang back to me and in harmony.

"Come, let's go up in the hills," I said one day. "There might be huckleberries still."

I rubbed Alice's hair, thick and black. If I thought too much about how she came to me, I feared she might go away again. It was an irrational fear, but I was getting used to that.

All of this was impossible, but by then many impossible things had already happened.

The next spring I birthed a second daughter, and Alice watched after her sister Belle. Alice had stopped growing when the top of her head reached the bottom of my chin, and I was not tall.

My second baby developed just as Alice had, and I ate voraciously to keep up her milk supply until, by autumn, they could feed themselves. And then another spring and another child was born, cared for by my second, and Alice returned to my side. At birth, each was smaller than any infant human I had ever known to survive, and each grew faster than was possible. I could not know at first that they would not live long, but I was not so foolish as to ignore how they were strange. I simply chose not to care how it had all happened.

By the time I had twenty daughters, the last year's child named Tina, Alice had borne a baby of her own. She was Ulla. I had not thought of my children as fully grown. I considered calling myself Grandmother, but they all called me Mother because Alice did. The next spring, only Vera was born to Belle, and I realized I had done birthing. Tina would be the last child born of my body. Now my daughters birthed.

Everything about their lives flowed quicker than mine.

They were clever with their hands, clever finding food, sometimes eating things I had never dared try. Perhaps their sense of smell was better. They rarely became ill from testing something they should not eat.

"Bad," said Alice once after spitting up on the ground before me. "Bad teffa," the girl said. She held out the frond.

"All right," I said. "We won't eat fern."

They ate skunk cabbage and other flowers and many roots, and they scraped the inner bark of downed trees and gathered seeds. Alice would sit beside me in the evening before she slept and tell me everything she'd seen and the other Daughters had done. They braided grasses and the chewed fibers of roots and reeds. They planted gardens of sorts, setting seeds in the center of a meadow east of the city and seeming to admire the plants as they grew. They invited the bees but did not steal honey, gathered dead wood but would not hurt a living tree.

I talked and talked to my daughters until I was hoarse, until I noticed they hardly spoke back. They sang.

One spring day, all the children, who mostly were not children at all anymore, but girls or little women, all wore crowns woven of new green leaves and trillium flowers. Alice put one of tiny dairies and wisps of seedheads around my head. They stood close to one another, close to me, wrapped their arms in a circle around me, and sang. New words, new notes, and they sang in harmony like a well-trained choir. I did not recognize the music at all. They grew beyond me, my Daughters. Even Alice, my oldest child, could not always explain to me the why or how of her living.

They wove little sacks of a particular reed, though I would not have known how to teach them. They wave baskets tight enough to carry water. Insects did not invade their stored seeds and dry berries. They taught me how.

Insects themselves seemed less common. While telling a story about the small, wee voice of Mosquito, I realized my Daughters had never seen a mosquito. Perhaps spiders had won? But spiders were no longer as common as they had been. It had been years since I walked into a web between trees.

My years were marked: a child was born, and walked for the first time, and began to sing. I deliberately named them alphabetically, each named for someone, until I accepted that they did not need names to know themselves, and it was hard sometimes for me to tell them apart.

Alice was my first and best child, the child of desperation and need. The rest of my children, like the first, came unbidden. I tried not to care too much about them and that was impossible.

The sound of my Daughters calling and singing above the less insistent whir and hiss of insect life was a background chorus.

Partway through the alphabet the second time, Alice died. Alice died, leaving twenty-six sisters, eleven nieces, and a daughter of her own. All of them Daughters but me.

I rocked the small body of my first born and wept and moaned. Daughters closed around. They held me steady when my body shook. They licked tears from my face.

The Daughters carried their sister, dug a place in the forest with a boulder as marker, and covered her with flowers before covering her in the earth. They sang the sun down. The song was about forest and fruiting trees, the berries that stained their fingers and the experiences of birth and birthing and falling away. Finally they fell away themselves and went on with life. I mourned and sat apart and useless.

All my singing children, all Daughters, and all their Daughters after them, were like that. Most years a birth and a death. I stopped counting and naming. Or rather, counted and named only for myself, recognized that there was no one else to whom most numbers or names mattered.

I cared for them automatically. Because I believed I should love them all the same, I tried, but it was my firstborn I had most wanted to keep safe. I tried not to care too much after Alice, because they would die too soon. I tried to love them all the same, or not to love them. I failed.

They did not cry, but often laughed. They waited patiently. They licked my hands and wrists less often than they licked one another's. Perhaps they recognized I did not like the gesture or need it as they seemed to themselves. They smiled and wrapped their arms around me and one another. They spoke, they sang the songs I taught them, but more often the ones they created themselves. I was content to have company.

How long did this idyll last? What were a few decades? My children grew, began to birth, and the oldest among them died while still young in my eyes. I had to let them go. I let them go.

Not sleeping—what was that about? Was it some kind of magical accommodation that allowed me to take 24/7 care of the girls? I wished I knew.

They slept. Sometimes they slept half the day if they were not busy gathering or making or working on something. I seemed only to drift.

Springtimes passed, and others came and left. Decades. Daughters born and birthing and passed. I was not alone. But by now I have lived too long.

There might be no one left on earth who remembers what I remember. The children listen, but probably do not believe the stories I tell, ordinary descriptions of feathers and clawed feet. Even to me, this feels like dreaming or fables, fanciful stories of babies crawling for months, the slow development of speech and years spent in school, birds flying and horses' muzzles velvety soft. Birdsong and frogs croaking and cows mooing. Dogs barking and cats mewing. Mice in the walls of houses. The eating of flesh, the sounds of a city. Open chest surgery. Libraries. Trains, planes, and automobiles. Illness and mourned death.

These are my stories—more like nightmare visions for which I claim nostalgia. Frightening by now even to myself. When I am gone, what will they preserve? While they remember what I say or sing, they write nothing. I have been unable to convince my progeny of the need for writing. Even to me, my stories sound fantastical. Dragons and sea monsters.

I think about Alice's laughter, my daughter's hand wrapped about my finger in the weeks after her birth, how by the following year Alice held the hand of Belle, and each youngest Daughter cared for the one after. I fed them, cleaned them, told them stories. I made decisions about where and when to move on. I was head of a large family. When did that change? My Daughters still move on without leaving me behind. They grow, become themselves and not merely a part of me. They walk into the forest and gather to sing, more than I can count. Over a hundred, and surely more gather to sing than come from my body. I never have more than forty-two Daughters alive at once. I try to count them again and cannot understand if I am counting them twice and three times or are there Daughters here who are not mine? It is another puzzle I cannot solve.

They sing a gift, not to me, but to one another. I follow them. The Daughters are well settled in their new world and have little need of me.

As if Alice stood before me, I hear her speak: "Mama." The voice in my head startles memory awake. One day long ago as we walked in this forest, Alice looked up into my eyes. "Mama, the other Mothers are tall like you."

"What other Mothers?"

She spun a leaf between her fingers, green like the glass. "There are nine Mothers in the world."

"How can you know there are others?" I said.

"Just nine," she said. "Far away." She sighed and smiled, and then went along humming.

The shard that cut my foot is green. A leaf color. What came in such bright green glass bottles? Soda? Wine? I hardly remember and it doesn't matter. I pull my foot up closer to my face to examine the wound. It is not so bad. I stand, test weight on my foot while turning the wounding glass in my fingers and rubbing its smooth outer side.

Here, I last held my firstborn. That first shocking birth and love of Alice is what I miss. Perhaps it is my lost usefulness. I have lived long past my time.

My living Daughters sing me back to the present. They are near. Like Alice did so long ago, they sing of other Mothers I will never know and other Daughters who join their choral gathering.

I am very tired. I half-close my eyes and give in to listening to their music, and when I open my eyes and look around, I find them waiting for my attention to return.

They smile. They stroke my hand. I worried for a long time about the end of the world, but the world does not end with me. I wonder if my Daughters think me a little mad.

Perhaps I am mad. Perhaps I will die now, because they are ready for me to leave them.

See Jan Priddy's story "All the Daughters Sing" online at Metaphorosis.
If you liked it, leave a comment. Authors love that!

Remember to subscribe to our e-mail updates so you'll know when new stories are posted.

About the story

This story began with an image of songbirds dropping from trees. (Rachel Carson talked about that happening due to the use of DDT in the 1950s. Dead birds on the ground. Eventually, she wrote *Silent Spring* and triggered the environment movement and the outlawing of DDT.) I did some research and found an island where that had happened—all the birds had died. Some plant species died out as a result. Then I went further: What if everything died? If birds died, reptiles are a cold-blooded relative and they would be dead. Amphibians were already in trouble. Where was the thundering croaking of frogs I used to hear in the wetlands nearby? And then large mammals are already dying out, so all mammals might die, and all humans. What if there were one survivor, the last person alive, how might life go on? No monsters, no rebuilding civilization, what if it was all gone and wasn't every going to come back? If fear of death is gone and competition and population pressure are removed from the human equation, what's left? What's essentially human about human beings? I wrote a long story about that last human being in 2018. And then, as I tried to shorten a novelette into a short story, it grew into a novella. And then, after Covid seemed to prove my premise more realistic than I'd known at the start, I took the NaNo challenge and rewrote my twenty-two thousand words as a full length novel. Then I set it aside because I was afraid to reread that draft... some day. Instead, I went back to the beginning and ground down and polished it to that five-thousand-word short story I'd been aiming for a few years back. It has gone through several titles, and I credit Molly Gloss for advising me to keep "All the Daughters Sing."

A question for the author

Q: How do you generate story ideas, and how soon do you act on them?

A: My stories often begin with something simple and familiar because of an experience I want to understand or an event in the world that triggers my curiosity. I ask myself "what-if" questions. And then I try to look at the world slant and think what could happen next. My education is all about creative work, but I am fascinated by science and history, what we understand, and what we fail to notice. I like the notion of one thing leading to another unexpected result. The friend whose neck was burned, the aunt who went to Peru, an owl dreaming, Schylar falls in love with Joan who loves Peter who loves Mark who loves Terry who sees Schylar run by one morning and follows right along behind. A draft might flow out in days. Getting the story right takes months or years. Even details I am certain are perfect, sometimes don't survive years of revision.

About the author

Jan Priddy began reading science fiction in high school when her father handed her Foundation, later earned undergraduate degrees in the visual arts from the University of Washington, and eventually studied writing with better authors including Ursula K. Le Guin and Molly Gloss. An MFA graduate from Pacific University, she lives in the NW corner of her home state of Oregon where she runs a couple of miles every other day. She weaves and bakes. She writes stories into the world.

janpriddyoregon.wordpress.com

My Little Sister Brigid

Harold R. Thompson

My little sister Brigid was born when I was four years old. I loved her from the start. She was this funny little pink smiley thing with a round bald head like a baseball, and for a while I called her Baseball Head. I enjoyed talking to her and telling her things, even if she didn't talk back. She never said a thing, even as she grew older. Our parents seemed worried, but I figured that was just the way she was. She would never speak and that was that. I played games and explained them to her. She just watched me with her huge eyes, and I thought she understood.

Once, after she'd returned from a trip to the doctor, I told her, "I'll make sure nothing bad ever happens to you."

I would make Mom and Dad happy and feel safe.

One day when she was five, Brigid looked at me and said, "What's for supper?"

"Pork chops and corn on the cob," I said. I'd been looking forward to that. Then I said, "Hey, you talked!"

After that she spoke in complete sentences worthy of any six-year-old, or even an adult.

"What are all those lines?" she asked me one day.

"What lines?"

She told me she could see gold shimmering lines in the air, like the edges of curtains, or giant sliced orange peels like you see in the marmalade. She even pointed to them, and traced them with a finger, but I couldn't see anything.

When Mom and Dad found out about the lines, off to the doctor they went. They were worried that Brigid had something wrong with her brain, something serious like a tumor. By then I was ten, and old enough to understand what that meant, so I was a little scared, but it turned out there was no sign of a tumor or any kind of disease. What the doctor had said, my parents told me, was that my little sister might have a type of 'spectrum disorder'.

The word 'spectrum' just made me picture a prism, and that made me think of the cover of Pink Floyd's *Dark Side of the Moon* album.

"Why is it called that?" I asked.

Dad's face scrunched up like he had a pain in his gut or something.

"It means," he said, "that she's different. Her brain works differently from other people's. Some parts are more developed and others are…"

I waited for him to finish the sentence, but he just looked away with that pained grimace.

"Are less developed?" I said.

I didn't believe that. I knew Brigid. My little sister was perfect. Some of my friends had annoying little sisters, but Brigid was never annoying. She didn't take my things. She watched my games and didn't interfere. She went away when I asked, plunked down in a corner with a book. She was only six, but always reading. She also followed instructions well. She said whatever was on her mind, so you always knew what she was thinking. She was curious and asked questions. She wanted to understand things.

But I worried about the lines in the air. That meant she was seeing things that weren't there.

I asked her about them again one night while we were in the den watching TV.

"Are there lines here now?" I asked.

"You still can't see them?"

"No, I can't. There aren't any lines, Bridge."

She glared at me, her pursed mouth looking like a button. Before my eyes, she reached out with one hand... and the hand disappeared.

I sat up on the couch. I rubbed my eyes. I wasn't sure what I was seeing.

"I just put my hand into one of the folds," she said.

Not lines anymore, but folds.

"There are things in here," she said.

Her hand reappeared, but now she was holding an old flashlight made of shiny aluminum. It had a red plastic cowl around the lightbulb, and a magnet on one side so you could stick it to the fridge. The plastic cowl was dirty and the shiny tube was dented in a few places.

"Where did that come from?"

Brigid shrugged.

"I saw one like it once. I thought of it and there it was. That's what the folds do, I think. I figured it out a few days ago. Look!"

She pulled out other things, one after the other: an adjustable wrench, a roll of masking tape, and a jar of peanut butter. I took the lid off the peanut butter to make sure it was real.

"It is," I said, after sticking in a finger and licking it clean.

This was a relief. My little sister hadn't been seeing things. The folds were real but just invisible. That meant she was going to be all right.

I got some bread from the kitchen and we ate some of the peanut butter with it.

A few days later, I went into Brigid's room to discover her playing with a huge castle made of coloured wooden blocks. Detailed plastic knights guarded the walls.

"Where'd you get all this?" I demanded, a little jealous.

Then I remembered what she could do.

"Oh, they came from the folds," I said.

Brigid ignored me and kept playing. She could be single-minded when she set herself to a task and would get upset if she was forced to deviate, even to answer a question.

It was after this that she started building elaborate Rube Goldberg machines. Most of them involved a steel ball rolling along a track, knocking things over and causing a chain reaction that would end with a fan turning on or a radio blaring or something. Some of the machines were huge, extending into the hallway and dining room and living room and even out the window. My parents were pretty tolerant of this, just like they'd tolerated the toy railroads I'd set up when I was Brigid's age, as long as she cleaned up after a few hours.

I don't know what went through my parents' heads when they found out Brigid could pull things out of thin air. When Dad first encountered one of the Rube Goldberg machines, he just told Brigid to put everything back when she was finished. But later I overhead them discussing the possibility of sending Brigid to a special school.

I was having none of that. I stormed into their bedroom.

"There's nothing wrong with Brigid!" I said. "She should go to our regular school."

Mom came over and put her hand on my shoulder.

"It's okay, it was just an idea," she said.

That was all.

I walked Brigid to school every day after that, and she always held my hand. After confronting my parents, I was pleased with myself for having saved her, in my mind, from having to attend some strange institution, but I also began to worry what others would think, including other students, even Brigid's teachers. I felt like I needed to stay close to her, to watch out for these potential villains.

"Remember," I said to her on her first day of Grade One. "Don't tell anyone about the folds or what you can do."

"I won't," she said. "But why not?"

"Just don't," I told her.

I didn't want to scare her with an explanation.

"The government is going to come and take her away," I said to my parents one night, and I got so upset I started to shake. A few tears even started. "They're going to want to do experiments on her."

My dad gave me one of his genuinely-concerned looks and put his hand on my shoulder.

"I don't think shadowy organizations like that really exist," he said. "This is a free democracy, and every citizen has rights. No one can just take you away against your will. If your little sister has special talents, that's her business and no one else's."

Did I mention my mom and dad were both lawyers?

As far as I could tell, Brigid never revealed her powers at school, and that was good, but as time passed, I started to worry that she wasn't really fitting in. Her schoolwork was perfect, straight As in every subject, but she didn't seem to make any friends. I'd see her in the playground by herself, sometimes just staring into space.

I wanted to change that.

"Why don't we have a big party?" I said to her one day when we were all sitting at the dinner table. "For your birthday. You can invite all the kids from your class."

Brigid gave me one of her stares, but after a moment she nodded.

"They would like that," she said.

We made paper invitations and invited about thirty kids. In those days, if someone in your class invited you to a party, no matter who it was, you'd go. It was only polite. Plus you got to go to a party. So on the big day, which was a Saturday, a ton of kids showed up, each one with a present, looking for fun and cake. I acted as host. Brigid meanwhile had made her largest Rube Goldberg machine yet, one that went through every room in the house, and it became the center of activities as every kid took a turn letting the steel ball drop.

When it was all over, Brigid said to me, "That was fun, having all those kids over."

"They're your friends," I reminded her.

"Are they? Oh."

After that, nothing changed. None of her classmates seemed to dislike her, and no one bullied her, but she still stuck to herself most of the time.

I'd tried. At least she would always have me, I figured.

As more time passed, and I turned thirteen (almost a man), I decided that it was good that my little sister was something of a loner. That was safer. I still worried, almost every day, that her secret would come out, and made a solemn pledge—a reaffirmation of my childhood promise—to protect my little sister from anyone who would try to do her harm or infringe her rights, as my dad had put it, as a citizen. I knew that if the powers-that-be found out what she could do, they would be afraid of her, and they would want to find out how her abilities worked so they could exploit them. That's what always happened in the movies.

Two more years passed and no one came to take Brigid away. In that time, I never let my guard down. If I saw a suspicious car parked on our street, I would check it out. I got in the habit of telling Brigid to hide whenever someone I didn't know came to the door.

"Why should I hide?" she asked me.

I finally decided to explain that there were people who could be afraid of her, or who wanted to use her for their own purposes, and make her do things she didn't want to do. I figured she was old enough to understand.

"But I'm just a nine-year-old kid," she said.

"You're different. Not everyone likes that."

That just made her frown.

When I was fifteen, my first year of high school, Brigid stopped eating her supper. Mom and Dad were worried she'd developed an eating disorder, but one day I caught her pulling a tray of cupcakes out of the air. She'd been snacking on magic goodies. She'd tried to hide it, even from me, and that made me angry. She and I weren't supposed to keep secrets.

I told Mom and Dad.

"You can't just eat cake and candy, honey," Mom said, and then she and Dad gave Brigid a lecture about what was right to pull out of the folds, what was wrong. They didn't mind the toys, but they didn't want her eating so much unhealthy food.

"Maybe it's time to get to the bottom of this," Dad said, "before it gets any more out of hand."

By that he meant another trip to the doctor.

"You can't do that," I said, horrified.

"We just want them to run a few tests, honey," Mom said. "We won't reveal everything, but... we just want to make sure she's okay."

I thought they were crazy and was sick to my stomach with worry. I wished I hadn't ratted on her. If the doctor found out what Brigid could do, he would just have to make one phone call, and the men from the government would be on our doorstep.

"Deny everything," I whispered to Brigid as she was leaving the house. "Tell the doctor it's just a game. It's not real."

Brigid just gave me one of her big-eyed looks.

I went into the back yard to wait, just sitting in a lawn chair and stared at the sky, at the clouds.

The back door opened and Brigid came out and sat in the chair next to mine.

"You're home already?" I said, startled.

My little sister shook her head.

"I did what you said and told Doctor Heppie that it was all a game, but he didn't believe me. I asked to go to the bathroom and then I decided to come home."

"What do you mean? Come home how?"

I felt a chill.

"I found a new way to use the folds," Brigid said.

I grabbed my phone and texted Mom, telling her what had happened. She'd been worried sick and the whole clinic had been running around trying to find Brigid.

"Thank you, honey," Mom wrote back. "Thank you for letting us know!"

When Mom and Dad got home, Brigid faced them and said, "Please don't take me to the doctor again."

I stood behind her, nodding.

"There's nothing wrong with her," I insisted.

Mom and Dad looked at me, then looked at Brigid.

"Okay," Dad said.

After this, I told myself I had to live by my own words, at least a little. I'd said there was nothing wrong with Brigid, but I behaved as if there was. My high-school friends knew I had a little sister, but I never invited anyone over because I was afraid they'd see Brigid do something, and then I'd have to explain. That had to change. I had to trust Brigid to be responsible, like she was at school. I told myself I had to start giving her more freedom.

One day I invited my friend Rosie over. I was learning guitar and Rosie played bass, and we were going to form a band to perform at the school music festival. This was going to be our first jam session, in our rec room.

Rosie wore her hair super short and also lifted weights, so she had rocks in her arms. She wore white t-shirts and jeans and that was the extent of her wardrobe.

"Are you a boy or a girl?" Brigid asked her, in her blunt way.

That embarrassed the hell out of me, but Rosie just laughed.

"A bit of both," she said.

"So you're just yourself," Brigid said. "Like me."

Rosie said nothing for a few seconds, then gave my sister a smile I can only describe as conspiratorial.

"Yeah."

I watched the two of them together, and something turned over inside me. I'd been carrying the secret of my little sister's power for a long time, and I needed some help with that weight, help from someone we could trust. I wondered if Rosie could be that person.

"My little sister is different from other people," I said.

I guess I was testing the waters. Brigid turned and looked at me with her big round eyes, and something in that look stopped me from elaborating.

Rosie shrugged.

"Everyone is different," she said. "Most people don't care about that stuff anymore."

Brigid smiled, and I felt a little burst of hope. Could that be true? Was it possible that few people, including the government, would really care if they found out what my sister could do?

I wanted to believe that, only Brigid didn't just have personality quirks, but actual powers.

I decided I'd have to carry the weight of my sister's secret for a while longer.

Not long after that, Brigid announced she wanted to have another birthday party. She was about to turn twelve and thought that was special. Her idea was to have a party where she gave the guests gifts instead of receiving them.

"Please don't give them things that you find inside the folds," I told her, worried that was her plan.

It was.

"Why not?" she asked. "Where else can I get the gifts?"

"Mom and Dad can buy them."

"But I want the gifts to be special."

Brigid trusted me and always listened to me, but I was spoiling her plans and she didn't like it.

"Look, I'm sorry about this," I said.

Brigid suddenly brightened.

"I know! I can say it's a game, like with the doctor. A magic trick! And I won't be lying, because it is a game, really. Right?"

I mulled this over. I was feeling pretty down about disappointing her, and this seemed like a reasonable compromise. If Brigid trusted me, I had to learn to trust her.

"Okay, but be careful," I said, hoping I wouldn't regret my decision.

At the party, Brigid revealed her power to all, telling the other kids that she could pull anything out of thin air. That's all she said. She didn't describe what happened as a magic act, but when it was over, everyone applauded. No one thought it was real. They deceived themselves.

I was proud of Brigid, both for her amazing talent and how she'd presented herself. But later that evening, my old fears started to filter back. What if a couple of the kids realized that what they were seeing was the real thing? What if they told their parents, and their parents called the police or some other authority?

On Monday morning, as I was packing a lunch for school, a large black truck pulled up to the front door. I told Brigid to hide in her room. The truck turned out to be a courier delivering a package for Mom, but I was shaken. I'd decided to walk Brigid to school like I used to do. I'd stopped when I'd moved to the high-school, and I'd probably be late for my first class, but my little sister's life was worth the wrath of my homeroom teacher.

When we arrived at the elementary school, a large black car was parked out front. A man in a black suit wearing Aviator sunglasses opened the driver's door and stepped out.

I'd never seen that car before. I led Brigid in a wide berth around it.

"You see that car?" I murmured in her ear. "I don't know for sure, but it looks like it might belong to those government guys who want to kidnap you. Stay away from them. Don't even let them see you."

Brigid gave me a big-eyed look and nodded.

"I don't want that," she said.

The passenger side door of the car opened, and a kid got out, a boy with a camouflaged knapsack. The man in the dark suit and sunglasses said something to the boy, who waved and started running toward the school.

"That's just someone's dad," Brigid said.

I watched as the man got back in the car, but he didn't drive away at once. Was he watching us? Had the kid with the knapsack been some kind of cover?

"I'm not sure," I said. "Don't talk to that kid or his dad. Okay?"

Brigid nodded.

"Okay."

I couldn't think of anything else the entire day and found it impossible to pay attention in class. I was terrified that the man I'd seen was a government agent who'd been sent to watch my sister. I wasn't certain, but that didn't matter. The idea had taken root and was growing.

I left my last class early, claiming to be sick. The truth was, I felt sick. I was so anxious, so worked up, I ran all the way to the elementary school and waited for Brigid to come out, all the while watching out for that black car.

When Brigid saw me she broke into one of her big smiles.

"Hi, big brother!"

She held my hand on the walk back, but neither of us said much. Brigid was still generally quiet, and I was busy keeping watch.

We were almost home when I saw a large black sedan turn onto our street. I came to a hard stop, jerking Brigid's arm.

"Ow!" she said.

I didn't know what to do for a few seconds, but there was nowhere to run.

"We have to keep going," I murmured.

I felt like I was walking in glue, but when we turned the corner, there was no black car on our street. Maybe it had just driven past.

On our front step, I knelt in front of Brigid and said, "I think I just saw that car again, and think it might have been looking for you. I think you should hide. Not just in your room, but... in the folds. Do you have a place to hide there?"

"Yes, I go there all the time," she said. "I can go there if you say so."

I didn't get my homework done that night, but sat in front of the window, plucking at my guitar and staring at the street. I didn't see the car again.

The next morning, Brigid wasn't at breakfast.

"Do you know anything about this?" Dad asked me. "Did she go to that place, wherever she goes?"

I shrugged. "I guess so."

I didn't want to admit I'd told her to go. I was afraid Mom and Dad would say I was being irrational.

"She'll come back," Mom said. "But we'll have to call the school and tell them she'll be absent today."

She was trying to sound casual, but I could tell she was upset, and felt a little pang. That was my fault.

I reminded myself that this was necessary.

Brigid still wasn't back when I got home from school, nor did she return the next day. Or the next. I started to get a little worried, and sat in her room and called her name, hoping she could hear me, but I had no idea how the folds worked. I told her I hadn't seen the black car for days and it was probably safe to come out. I even felt a little stupid, and had to admit that maybe I'd been wrong.

By now Mom and Dad were a wreck, but they couldn't go to the police. Their daughter wasn't missing. They knew exactly where she was.

"What if she stays away forever?" Dad said at a joyless supper on that third day.

Mom reached out and took his hand.

"We always knew something like this could happen," she said. "She's unique.

She's special, and she's just flexing those muscles. Why would she stay away forever? Don't worry about that."

My Dad just nodded. I'd never seen him cry before, but tears started running down his cheeks.

That night, I came down with a fever. I don't know if it was due to raw negative emotions or if I'd let myself get worn down and the flu had taken the opportunity to attack. When the sun rose the next day, I couldn't get out of bed. The room spun when I tried to raise my head, and I think I had visions. I saw Brigid standing next to me and asked her where she'd been.

"Come on," I heard her say, as if from a distance.

I managed to sit up. Brigid was right next to me, but half of her seemed to be missing, like she was peering around a curtain. Or a fold.

"Follow me," she said, voice a whisper.

She slid back behind the fold, but held out her hand. It looked like her severed arm was floating in the air.

I took her hand and let her guide me through the fold in space.

On the other side was a room, like an ordinary room in a house, though with no features, the floor, walls, and ceiling all resembling white plaster. In the far wall was an ordinary wooden panel door with a white doorknob. Next to the door stood a massive palace of wooden blocks, like I'd seen Brigid build years ago, its walls armed with plastic cannon. In another corner was a table covered in maps drawn in coloured pencil, and beside them were the remains of hamburger wrappers and cupcake papers. Books were stacked in little piles here and there.

Brigid let go of my hand.

"How do you like it?" she said.

"It's... nice."

My head was starting to clear and I could see there was a certain coziness to the room. It couldn't have been more safe, more secure, but I hated the idea of my sister spending her life like this, hiding from the world that was rightfully hers.

I wanted her to come home.

"Bridge, I think I might have been wrong," I said. "I haven't seen the car again, and no one came to look for you. I think the coast is clear and you need to come back. Mom and Dad are worried."

She looked at me.

"They are?"

She said it like it had never occurred to her.

"Yes."

"But they know where I went."

"They want you to come home. You don't really need to hide all the time."

She looked at me, eyes big.

"I'll keep you safe," I promised for the thousandth time.

She nodded.

"Okay, I believe you. You always tell me the truth."

I digested this as she went to the panel door and grabbed the doorknob. The door swung open, and beyond was the rec room in our house.

"Can I step through?" I said.

"Yes! Just follow me."

When I'd gone through the doorway, I looked behind me, but all I saw was the other wall of the rec room. The door and Brigid's hiding space were gone.

I felt like I'd just awakened from a dream. The fever was gone and there was my little sister, standing next to me and smiling. Safe and sound.

"What time is it?" I said. I'd been home alone, sick in bed, and something about the light coming in the high rec room windows said it was late, afternoon coming on to evening. School would be out.

"I don't have a clock in my hiding place," Brigid said. "Maybe I should get one?"

I wanted to check the street one last time, just to make sure.

"Come on," I said.

We went out through the basement door and up the concrete steps to ground level. Our driveway was empty, and I looked along our street to the left, at all the other quiet semi-suburban houses, each with its garage or car port, front lawn and shrubs and flower beds.

There were no black cars and no one was trying to take my sister away.

"I guess I'll have to go to school tomorrow," Brigid said. "And everyone will say, oh, where were you? Welcome back. It'll be like a party."

"And even if we told them where you'd been," I said, "they wouldn't believe us."

I smiled at her, and in that moment, I made my decision, the decision I'd been building towards. It was time for me to let go of the fear for good. And this time I meant it.

"You know when I said I'd keep you safe?" I said. "I'll still try, but I don't think you'll need me. You can keep yourself safe."

"You think so?"

"Yes."

I looked again at the empty street.

"You know what else?" I added. "Mom and Dad will be home later, and they're going to be happy to see you."

In this I was wrong. Mom and Dad weren't happy. They were overjoyed.

"You didn't have to worry," Brigid told them.

I watched as they enveloped my little sister in a three-way hug. I joined in.

They say old habits die hard, and over the next few months and even into Brigid's high school years, I secretly watched for black cars. I never saw one, and I never talked about them.

I did my best to stick to my decision.

After her senior year, Brigid won a scholarship to a reputable university and I faced my biggest test. Could I stand it, with my little sister away from home, living in a dorm?

Turns out I could. I kept waiting for something terrible to happen, but it never did. One weekend she came home, traveling through the folds, and told me, "I think I'd like to be an architect. I like to design and build things."

"That sounds like you," I said.

A few months later, she told me, "I'm going to switch to engineering. I like to design and build things, but all kinds of things, not just buildings."

She was a star pupil, which came as no surprise. After graduation, she got a job in another city.

Her visits became fewer.

We were both busy, but still made time for each other. By then I had two kids, six and three, and Brigid delighted in entertaining them with her 'magic tricks' when she came to dinner.

"I'm not sure I'm going to make it next week," she told me one evening, when the plates had been cleared from the table and we were alone for a few minutes. "Things are getting crazy and I might have to put in some extra hours."

"You do what you have to do," I told her. "And you know where to find me."

As it turned out, I didn't see her the next week, nor the week after. One day she sent me a text message. She was in town for business, and could I meet her for coffee? Not could she come to the house, but a coffee date. Just for an hour or so.

I was a little disappointed, but agreed to meet her.

I arrived at the coffee shop first and grabbed us a table. Brigid came in a few minutes later, tall and slender and grinning. She still wore her hair long, almost down to her waist.

We didn't talk about anything significant. We just chatted about what was going on in our lives. At one point, I wanted more cream for my coffee, and Brigid pulled a little porcelain pitcher out of the folds. It was casual and surprising, and no one seemed to notice.

"Do your work colleagues know you can do that?" I asked.

"They see it all the time. Everyone still thinks it's a trick. They don't believe it's real."

I leaned back in my chair. I wanted to ask something that I'd wondered about for a while.

"Do you... ever feel tempted to reach into the folds and grab a few bags of cash?"

Brigid's big eyes seemed to double in size and her jaw dropped open.

"That wouldn't be fair!" she said. "And how would I explain that on my tax returns?"

"Well, you've never been reluctant to find us presents in there!"

Brigid shook her head.

"That seems different somehow. I think I make those things. You're not allowed to make your own money."

I could think of a few counter arguments but kept them to myself. Her response was typical for her, and I felt myself flush with love and admiration.

"Sometimes I think I should go to the physics department at the university," she continued, "and show them what I can do and say, what do you think? But then you know how much I value my privacy. I don't need them trying to figure me out. And that's not who I am anyway. I'm not really that interested. I've got other fish to fry."

She sipped her coffee. We talked about other things. Eventually she checked her watch and said, "I'm sorry I have to dash, but I'll see you at Thanksgiving. You're going to Mom and Dad's?"

I was, and I would see her there.

We embraced, and then she was out the door. I watched her walk away, back to the life she had chosen, and wondered if, after all, we had become a little ordinary. I'd read once that extraordinary children often became ordinary adults.

Well, I decided that was a crazy thought, and turned away, smiling to myself. Completely crazy. If there was one thing I'd learned, after all these years, after all the worries and reliefs, all the failures and triumphs, there was nothing ordinary about my little sister Brigid.

See Harold R. Thompson's story "My Little Sister Brigid" online at Metaphorosis.
If you liked it, leave a comment. Authors love that!
Remember to subscribe to our e-mail updates so you'll know when new stories are posted.

About the story

This was an unusual story for me, because normally I plan everything before I start actually writing and take my time building the story, layer by layer. I like to know the ending before I begin. However, this one came to me out of nowhere while I was making a cup of tea in the kitchen. I don't know where the name Brigid came from, but I was thinking of my childhood, about growing up with an older sibling, and of my own children and their relationship, and just tossed in a "what if" element. I sat down at my laptop and wrote the first draft from start to finish as a sort of stream of consciousness piece. No planning, no plot outline. It took me about an hour. Many of my short stories have both a horror element and a lot of action, but this was just the story of a little girl with extraordinary powers and an overprotective brother. It was a bit like a superhero origin story, but I wanted it to be about two kids growing up, not an action piece. I'd just been reading a collection of Kelly Link stories, and although my piece was nothing like what she writes, there was some influence. I didn't do much revision after that first draft, and shopped it around for a while, and it actually made several short lists, but I was never happy with the ending and neither was anyone else. Eventually, after some suggestions from the editor of this publication, I took another look and wrote several revised drafts. The ending was still the problem, but as I put myself back into the lives of those characters, it eventually revealed itself, as most endings do.

A question for the author

Q: Is there a specific environment you find most conducive to writing, and is it different for different kinds of scenes?

A: I write on a laptop, so I change venues quite a bit. It doesn't really matter where I go. That being said, I do most of my writing, and certainly my best, in the evening, or in the middle of the night. The silence, the lack of distractions from work and family, really helps, but my brain also slips into a more creative mode in the wee hours. It doesn't matter what kind of scene I'm writing. If I get stuck, the place that helps me get unstuck is... the shower. Some people sing in the shower, but I think. Maybe something about that environment helps me focus, again shutting out everything else, but it always seems to work, like magic.

About the author

Harold R. Thompson enjoys storytelling in all its forms. A long-time employee of Parks Canada, he develops exhibits and public programming at several national historic sites. He also writes historical fiction and science fiction and fantasy, both short stories and novels. He lives in Nova Scotia with his family.

haroldrossthompson.com

River's Song

Michael Barron

Boxes form a solid wall in the back of the SUV, preventing me from getting one last look at our house. I squeeze myself against the seat, head resting against the cool November glass, hugging my guitar. I'll never play the guitar again. After tonight I'll never even hear a guitar again. They don't have music where we're going.

Dad and I spent the weekend packing, but that was all a show for the neighbors. Just before midnight tonight, everything in the SUV — my phone, my old American Girl dolls, both my high school yearbooks, even Dad's precious tablet — is going in a furnace in New Jersey.

We pass the church where I attended Girl Scouts as a kid and then the train station where one January morning Emily and I huddled, trying to keep warm. The plan was to skip school and spend the day visiting comic book stores across Manhattan — because that's the kind of rebels we were. But when the train rounded the corner, all our rebelliousness evaporated and we scampered off to AP Chemistry.

If I'd known this day was coming so soon, I would've climbed aboard.

As we cross the Pine River Bridge, officially leaving my hometown forever, Dad glances at me out of the corner of his eye. "If it were up to me, you could come back to visit. However, they cannot send someone on a whim. You know that."

I do know that. Our civilization has generated faster than light travel, technology that can fling consciousnesses across the galaxy, artificial bodies in which to store those consciousnesses, and — according to Dad — breathtaking works of art, awe-inspiring architecture, and a flawless legal system. However, they still have a budget to consider.

I hold up my hand, wiggling my fingers. I'd never realized how much I adored my fingers until Dad delivered the news just a couple weeks ago. When he called me into the kitchen, I'd assumed he wanted to discuss the town's new recycling schedule. Instead, he gave a smile that actually reached his eyes and said, "We are going home."

Sitting at the kitchen table, a dull ache pressed against my side, nearly doubling me over.

"And it will not just be us. Uncle Trench and Coral are also being called back. We—"

"No." The word leapt out with such conviction I startled myself.

Dad's smile barely wavered. "River—"

"We've only been here eleven years. You said we'd have twenty-five."

"I never said that."

"Yes you did." I leaned across the table, my elbow knocking over the black cat pepper shaker I'd set out for Halloween. "After I started second grade and all the kids were mean to me, you took me to the aquarium to cheer me up. You complained the whole time about how dull ocean life is here. I asked how much longer we had to stay and you said we'd be 'stuck here for *at least* twenty-five years.' "

Dad clearly doesn't remember this. "You were not meant to take me literally."

"How was I supposed to know that?" I press my back against the chair and cross my arms. "I'm not going. I'll live with Emily or one of the other families, but I'm staying."

Dad didn't yell. He never yelled, the same way he never laughed, cried or got frustrated. He simply put the pepper shaker back where it belonged, scooped up the black specks until everything was nice and tidy and walked out of the room. "Families belong together, River. And neither of us belongs here."

The night after dad's big announcement, the nightmare came again. I knew it would. Whenever we talked about going back, my one memory of home always interrupted my sleep.

In my one memory, Dad and I swam upwards, faster than I'd ever swum before. Others rocketed past. A white tower loomed overhead. Half of Dad's appendages — people here would call them "tentacles" but I hated that word — clung to me. The rest thrashed as we flew higher, toward the ocean's surface. I'd never been to the surface before. The lack of pressure made me dizzy. Sunlight blinded me. Something far below wanted to kill us.

There was a flash of white light, not from the surface but from the tower. The structure began to crumble. Debris hurtled toward us. Dad veered to the left, but something struck my side. I thrashed in his arms. I was just a kid, barely old enough to form memories, but I remember thinking, *this is how I die.*

I woke soaked in sweat, still able to see the imploding tower in the darkness. The side of my human body ached.

Breathing in through my nose and out through my mouth, I crawled from bed, crept down the hall, turned on all the bathroom lights — even the one in the closet — and pulled up my Joni Mitchell T-shirt. No blood. No shredded skin. Only a handful of moles and one fat nuclear-red pimple, nothing to indicate I'd ever been near a warzone. But the pain remained, crossing thousands of lightyears, passing black holes and supernovas just to stab me between the ribs.

When I was a kid, I'd ask Dad if my real body had been injured during the explosion. This was back when I still referred to my original body — the one waiting for me in storage on our home world — as my 'real' body. He always shook his head at the question. "After the Citadel was destroyed, I took you straight to the medical domes. I waited for news of your condition along with thousands of others who were waiting for word of their own loved ones. When they released you, you came swimming out, happy as can be, with only the tiniest of scars." He'd hold up his thumb and forefinger to indicate how miniscule the scar was. Each time they'd be closer and closer together, as if my injury shrank with each retelling.

Dad had less to say when I asked, "Why'd the Citadel blow up?"

"It was a stupid, unnecessary tragedy caused by the Red Ocean Brotherhood, but don't worry about them. They're a joke."

"Who are they?"

Dad always swatted that question away as if he were swatting a fly. He preferred to dwell on our home world's brilliant architecture, glorious history, and yearly festivals in which every member of our species gathered together to create a single work of art. It sounded like a combination between a play and an unbelievably intricate live action role playing campaign.

It was my cousin Coral who told me all about the Red Ocean Brotherhood. She wasn't my biological cousin, just the daughter of Dad's favorite co-worker. One January evening when I was in the fourth grade, Coral and I were hanging out in the backyard, watching the snow fall, while Dad and Uncle Trench sat in the living room playing music on Dad's tablet. Without any precursor I turned to her and asked, "What is the Red Ocean Brotherhood?"

Dad's bosses had placed Coral's consciousness in a body that appeared to be two years older than mine. She was more than happy to lecture me on things she thought I should know. "They're an evil group that thinks everything involving dry land is 'blasphemous'. A bunch of them used to be teachers or politicians, even some scientists, but they swam off into the deepest channels when we started moving to the continents. They think everyone who lives on dry land deserves to die."

"Are they still around?"

"Of course they are." Before I could ask any follow up questions, she began to lecture me on how I should give up the guitar and stop listening so much to music created by mammals, leaving me to wonder what the Red Ocean Brotherhood would do to someone who'd spent her whole life on dry land.

I sit in a Burger King off I-95 nursing a Pepsi and a box of chicken tenders. This is our last meal on earth and it's fast food. Someone who doesn't know Dad would think he'd go for a five-star restaurant, but he can't tell the difference between Italian Cuisine and movie theater nachos. If it doesn't remind him of the sea plants back home, it's trash.

I stare at my fingers and wonder if my body will still feel pain when my consciousness leaves it. They recycle all the organic material after we go home. Soon my fingers might be a part of the inner thigh of a middle-aged man or the arm flab of an elderly woman.

The only other customers in the restaurant are a mother and her daughter, who looks like she might be about four or five. That's how old my body appeared to be when I first arrived. They share a milkshake while the mother lists all the relatives and the relative's pets they'll see at Thanksgiving. The girl has a chocolate grin smeared across her face.

I'm lucky. I know I'm lucky. At exactly midnight tonight I'll step through a door and my consciousness will be flung across the vastness of space. I'll wake in a technological utopia where I'll torpedo through our underwater metropolis in my new — 'real' — body, experience wonders I cannot imagine, and participate in the yearly festival that unites our species.

Of course before I'm able to speak with anyone, I'll have to master a form of communication that involves seventy-eight appendages instead of one mouth. I'll have to alter my perspective on what's tactful, beautiful, and funny. By the time I'm hanging out with friends again, I'll have to — for the second time in my life — become a member of an entirely new species.

The first of us arrived to this world in an actual craft. Apparently somewhere in the wilds of North Dakota, a silver sea shell lies in the middle of a field, marking our initial landing spot.

Sorry it's not in Roswell, New Mexico.

Over the years our people — their consciousnesses transferred into human bodies, of course — formed a fake company that bought a derelict factory off the New Jersey Turnpike. In the factory's sub-basements, they used parts of our original craft to construct vats where they grew even more human bodies as well as the gateway that sends and receives consciousnesses.

I remember nothing of what it was like to have my essence transmitted from one end of the galaxy to the other. After the attack on the Citadel, my next clear memory is of waking in a human body, ten fingers, and ten toes, and as far as I knew that was normal.

For months, Dad and I received lessons in how to walk, move objects with our hands, and communicate. They eased us in, first teaching us American Sign Language before moving on to verbal communication. Dad struggled; he never stopped struggling. After each lesson he'd go back to our room and sit hunched over on the edge of his bed, like a man who needed to scream, but had forgotten how.

I, however, was so young, I picked up these new languages overnight. By the time they moved us into the one-story bungalow that would be our new home, I was fluent in ASL, English, and Spanish. And of course I used these new communication skills to do what all little kids do: I asked questions.

"Where do the stars go in the daytime?"

"Why do we always have kale for dinner?"

"When can we get a dog?"

But my favorite question was, "Why're we here?"

Dad always answered with, "We are here to observe a land-based society so we might study their infrastructure and spread civilization to the terrestrial regions of our own world."

That answer never satisfied me. The aliens on TV were always flying around in spaceships, either destroying or saving the galaxy. Dad had traveled lightyears for a desk job.

But the job was his life. He exhausted himself studying highways, skyscrapers, communication networks, and sewers, complaining the whole time that the buildings back home were more 'inspiring'. And at the end of the day, when his work was finally done all he wanted to do was play music on his tablet.

While I grew up watching *Avatar: The Last Airbender* and *Star Wars Rebels* — which taught me how *real* aliens were supposed to act — the only entertainment Dad enjoyed came from an app Uncle Trench had programed himself.

When you opened the app, the bottom third of the screen was filled with seventy-eight gold symbols, our entire alphabet. Depending on which combination he pressed, different colors exploded, merged or swirled about. Our bodies back home barely detect sound, but we have enormous eyes that turn the ocean's bioluminescent twilight into high noon. What Dad was doing was our equivalent of playing music.

The 'song' he enjoyed the most began with a midnight-blue fog and turquoise shimmers running along the edges. Silver flecks swam through accompanied by emerald tendrils. Eventually, a single blazing light appeared in the heart of the fog, filling the screen with a golden glow.

This formation of colors was similar to a folk or gospel song, along the lines of 'Amazing Grace'.

Every Sunday morning he'd sit me down at the kitchen table and watch me practice. The routine began on the very first Sunday after we moved into the house and didn't stop until the day Dad told me we were going home. "This is far more cultured than that auditory trash the mammals hammer out on their instruments." I'd nod in agreement, just to placate him.

Every once in a while he'd share a story about how before we came here he'd once played his favorite song in our medical domes' waiting area. "Occasionally one of the doctors would emerge, take someone aside, and it would either be good news or bad. It was almost always bad. Eventually the waiting became unbearable, people became agitated, arguing with one another. And so, at last, I pulled out my..." He shakes his head. "This clumsy mouth cannot pronounce the word. I pulled out the musical instrument this app is based on. I sat in the middle of the crowd and began to play. People turned to watch. They stopped arguing and gathered together, focusing on my music, and after a while the crowd became one family again."

Sometime in middle school I realized he was telling me a story about what had happened after the attack on the Citadel. But as a kid it was just another boring story.

Between his nostalgic ramblings and the musical instrument that meant nothing to me, it was a relief when, eighteen months after we first arrived, Dad's bosses insisted that I attend public school.

On my first day of second grade, Dad walked me to the bus stop, wringing his hands, reminding me I could call whenever I needed to. Meanwhile, I skipped along beside him, confident that by the end of the day I'd be best friends with everyone at the school.

By lunch, I realized that most of the kids already had enough friends and didn't want to have anything to do with me. Throughout that first week, I smuggled in candy to share with the other kids. This worked fairly well for a few days, but before long they'd just snatch the offered Milky Way bars and run off to whisper and stare at me from across the playground.

After school I'd look into the bathroom mirror while holding up photos of kids in magazines, trying to determine what was wrong with me. Did my skin look too artificial? Could they see something alien in my eyes? Maybe there was some kind of subliminal anomaly that clued people in that I didn't belong, the way rats can tell when one of their own is diseased.

I got into the habit of leaving school through a side entrance, to avoid the other kids. Even their parents didn't hide the way they stared at me. One day, just a couple of weeks before winter break, I was walking down the side stairwell, which I assumed was empty, when I heard giggling coming from one floor above me. I refused to look up, which was a good thing because an instant later something thick and slimy splattered against the top of my head, like I'd been hit by a pint-sized bird dropping.

Even when I saw that my hands and hair were bright green, I didn't comprehend what had happened until the giggling turned to laughter followed by a stampede. There had to have been at least five of them. Five kids hated me so much they'd stolen a jar of paint, and lain in wait to ambush me. And the color they'd chosen...

It was the holidays. There had probably been some green paint lying around, but my mind leapt to: *little green men.* They knew what I was.

I ran. I didn't know where I was running to but I sprinted as fast as I could, face stinging from tears. I reached the bottom of the stairwell, swung a left, and burst into the closest bathroom.

I tried to dunk my hair under the sink but it was too shallow. I cupped my hands and attempted to wash it out, convinced that if anyone saw me smeared with green paint they'd realize I didn't belong on this planet. However, each scoop of water just spread the paint. Before long the walls, mirrors, and floor were splattered green.

The paper towel dispenser was empty so I hurried to the stalls to grab some toilet paper. That was when I noticed that one of the doors was shut.

Before I could decide whether or not I should just go, sprint all the way home, a girl's voice quivered, "Go away."

I almost did leave, but there would still be hundreds of people in the parking lot, ready to point and laugh.

"Please!" she said. "Just leave me alone."

I dropped to the floor, dripping green water across the tiles, and peered under the stall's door. I saw a pair of white sneakers and jeans splattered with mud.

"They're all out of paper towels," I told her.

"I know." She started sobbing louder.

"What's wrong?"

After a few minutes of prompting I got her to share her story. "I was carrying my art project — this giant painting I made of a robot dragon — down the gym steps when a gust of wind blew it out of my hands. I tried to catch it, but I slipped and fell into some mud in front of *everyone*. When I stood up Rodney Dickerson said I'd s-h-i-t myself. Even his mom laughed."

"If it makes you feel better, some kids dumped green paint into my hair."

"Really?" there was a tinge of curiosity in her voice.

"Yeah, that's why the floor looks like a leprechaun puked all over it."

"Gross!" she laughed.

We both grew quiet for a moment and then she asked, "Can I see your green hair?"

"Um..." I stepped back. "I guess."

The stall door swung open.

She was a petite girl with long black hair. I recognized her from the other second grade class, but she was so quiet I'd hardly ever noticed her.

To her credit, when she saw my green hair she did try to stifle her laughter, but the more she kept it in, the pinker her face became, which got me giggling. At last we both burst into laughter, and kept on laughing while she took me over to the sink and helped me wash my hair.

Nine years later, Emily and I dyed our hair green to commemorate the way we'd met.

Six months after that, Dad called me into the kitchen to tell me we were going home.

We're late for the rendezvous. Dad drives thirty miles over the speed limit, twisting the steering wheel with each turn like he's going to rip it from the dashboard. I want to point out that we still have over an hour until midnight, but the only thing that'll calm him is to get there.

When we finally reach the factory's rusting gate, he crashes through, not caring what kind of damage he does to the SUV. The high beams illuminate the ancient building. The parking lot is covered in so much shattered asphalt we might as well be driving across a gravel road. About fifty of Dad's colleagues wait for us on the far side. Everyone is there; even a few from the Hong Kong unit have flown in to give him a proper send off.

As soon as the SUV is parked, I expect him to leap out and get to work burning our possessions, but he remains in his seat, staring at the crowd.

"Dad?"

He doesn't look at me when he says, "We don't belong here, River. Once we get home our real lives will begin." Dad opens the door and climbs out. I remain where I am for several beats of my artificial heart. In his eyes, nothing that's happened to me counts as 'real life.'

But we're here now. There's nothing left for me to do but glance over my shoulder, give all of our boxed possessions, everything I've accumulated over the years, one last look, and pull myself out of the car.

As we approach the crowd, I take in the surrounding parking lot, the broken bottles, the cracked chunks of pavement, my final view of home.

Then my eyes fall on the others. Something's wrong. They should be clustered together, applauding, cheering, peering through telescopes, searching for our star. Instead, they're scattered. A few huddle in groups of two or three, but most are solitary.

Coral leans against the factory's bay doors, her pale face illuminated by the sickly orange streetlights. She should be leaping up and down, spitting on the ground, shouting about leaving this 'rock' forever. Instead, her bloodshot eyes glare, as if she's trying to crush me beneath her scowl.

Dad still hasn't noticed anything out of the ordinary. He walks with a skip in his step.

Uncle Trench meets us halfway across the parking lot. "I tried calling you."

"I left my phone at a hamburger restaurant." Dad grins, certain that nothing will ruin his day. "I never want to use that abomination again."

Trench speaks so quietly it's as if he doesn't want to hear his own words. "We received a communication. There was an attack... The Red Ocean Brotherhood..."

He falters, lowering his head. "Much of the city has been… We've lost contact."

The sugary, acidic aftertaste of the Pepsi I had with dinner coats my tongue. The frigid night air is impossible to breathe. I can't take my eyes off Dad.

He wavers back and forth, as if he's about to tip over. "Red Ocean is a joke."

Trench lowers his eyes. "It seems we may have underestimated them."

"How much damage?"

"We don't know, but…the storage facility, where they kept our bodies… It's not looking good."

Uncle Trench and I barely catch Dad before he tumbles to the cracked asphalt. Others step forward, but the only one who reaches us in time to help is Coral. As she takes his shoulders, she whispers to me, "Guess you got exactly what you wanted."

"Your cousin's kind of a bitch," Emily said behind me.

"Yeah." I rummaged through the fridge looking for the leftover tofu curry I was going to heat up for dinner.

We'd just run into Dad, Uncle Trench, and Coral in the driveway. Emily and I were coming back from the park where the small ragtag group of friends we'd accumulated over the years had been making plans to go to the New York Comic Con in October. Dad and the others didn't bother telling us where they were heading off to. As they passed, Dad and Uncle Trench gave us cordial waves, but Coral walked straight through Emily, knocking her to the ground.

"My whole family is weird," I said, pulling out the leftovers.

"Bet they're not as weird as my family," Emily said, wandering into the living room. "What's this?"

Before I could turn, my phone buzzed. It was a text from Uncle Trench.

Your father left his instrument hooked up to the projector.
He wants you to put it away.

The leftovers splattered all over the counter as I sprinted into the living room.

A reddish orange glow reflected off Emily's face. She gripped Dad's tablet, pressing random characters, so the projector cast fireballs across the wall. "Is this some kind of art app?"

"It's nothing!" I rushed at her so fast I slammed my shin against the coffee table. Stifling curses, I said, "It's just some dumb game my dad plays."

She pressed her palm flat against the keyboard, hitting all seventy-eight characters at once. The projection became a deafening cacophony of crimson, amber, indigo, violet, and silver. "How do you play?"

"You don't 'play' it. It's like a visual musical instrument. Never mind, it's stupid."

"It's incredible." She continued to experiment with the buttons.

I reached out to snatch the tablet away, but she was having so much fun I ended up lowering my hands and stepped back to watch her play.

One way or another I showed her how to play the first tune Dad ever taught me, our equivalent of 'Twinkle, Twinkle Little Star'. Blue and silver sparks flashed across the screen. Emily got the hang of it soon enough and we moved on, messing around with the various chords Dad had taught me over the years, even his favorite, the midnight blue with a golden glow.

Within a couple of hours, I discovered a combination I was particularly interested in. Silver orbs rained down the screen. When one hit the bottom, it turned green and flew about. As I watched that little green drop twirl among the others, something shifted inside me, as if the colors and images had a voice, and I finally understood what they were saying.

Eventually, Emily's mom texted telling her it was time to come home. I put the projector and the tablet away and we never played it again. However, at least twice a week for the next month, I'd crawl out of bed in the middle of the night and play the tune we'd discovered. I only stopped after Dad told me we were going home.

Uncle Trench, Coral, and I settle Dad onto the broken parking lot. Dad lays flat on his back, as if the gravity of this world pins him there. Everyone else stands apart in their little clusters. Eventually, they return to staring up at the stars, half of which are blocked by the factory looming overhead.

I don't know which of the stars is ours, even though Dad pointed it out to me countless times. Ever since I woke in the factory's sub-basement, I'd known I would someday return, that someday I'd see the underwater metropolis and all the art and beauty our people had to offer. Every time Dad described our civilization over kale salads or made me play songs on his tablet, he was promising I'd someday be a part of it. Now I might never swim among the towers or see the hundreds of miles of murals or any part of our world.

I don't realize how silent the night is until Uncle Trench says, "They might be able to grow new bodies for us. But that will take years, decades if the facility has been severely damaged. And if they need to start everything over from scratch, they may need to send an actual craft to assist with our end of the gateway. I don't even know if they have the budget for..." His voice drifts off as he shakes his head.

Dad pulls himself up and presses both hands against his face. "How many are dead?"

"We don't know. The area they attacked was densely populated, they—"

"Red Ocean is a joke." There's a quiver in his voice, but there's also an insistence, as if he's trying to assert that this is an objective statement.

I rest a hand on Dad's shoulder. He lowers his hands and turns toward me. I have to stop myself from looking away. There's just enough light from the streetlamp for me to make out his features, and I'm not ready to see his red tear-streaked face. I don't want to see the same accusation Coral shot me. *"Guess you got exactly what you wanted."*

But his face is as emotionless as the factory's brick wall. Without looking at me he says, "You need to get somewhere warm. These bodies are so delicate." He pulls himself to his feet. "I'll call Emily's mother. Explain our travel plans have been... That you will be staying with them for a while."

"Where will you be?" I stand up next to him.

"I'm needed here."

"Doing what?"

He doesn't answer, but I can already see him burrowed deep in the bowels of the factory, staring at our gateway, willing it to flicker to life and for all of this to be a silly misunderstanding. Dad walks toward the factory. "I'm needed here, River."

I step back. Coral isn't wrong. This is what I wanted. Within twenty-four hours I'll be back at one of my friend's houses, making extra spicy nachos while having unapologetically geeky conversations about music and comics. I should be performing a mental jig, struggling not to grin from ear to ear that my life will not have to change. However, instead I find myself staring at the others scattered about, and I feel the old pain press against my side. Right now, at this exact moment, the Red Ocean Brotherhood is reaching across the vastness of space and hurting us, just like they did with the Citadel.

I think of the Citadel and consider the story my dad told me. I burst into a run.

"Is she ditching us already?" Coral asks, loud enough for everyone to hear.

I run across the cracked asphalt until I reach the SUV. Dad didn't bother closing the driver's side door. I leap inside. Crawling into the back I work my way through a conglomeration of clothes, old toys, books, and everything else that made up our lives. At last, I find what I'm looking for in a small white tub.

By the time I pull myself out of the car, Dad has nearly reached the factory's bay doors. He walks as if there is no life above his waist. He's ready to slump over before the gateway and stare into the shadows beyond the dead gray metal, waiting for a response that will never come.

I open the white tub, place his projector on the SUV's hood and flick it on, connecting it with his tablet. "Wait!" I shout. "Look!"

He turns as I open the app, illuminating his face with the two-story square of light cast against the factory's wall. I hit a random gold character.

Colors explode.

For a moment all I produce is a mad cacophony of oranges, reds, and golds. Then I really begin to play, tapping the chords Dad had me practice every Sunday morning for eleven years.

It isn't perfect. I've never been talented at playing Dad's music. At first the blues are too light. Then they're too purple. At last I find the perfect shade of midnight. A turquoise aura seeps around the edges. Silver flecks dart this way and that among emerald tendrils. A sunshine-yellow glow emerges from the heart of the deep blue fog.

One by one, Uncle Trench, Coral, and the rest turn. Red eyes blink in the projector's light. Even more of us emerge from the shadows, making their way across the parking lot. Wrapping their arms around each other, they gather in close, as if the light provides actual warmth.

There are not enough silver flecks and the golden glow still holds a hint of mustard, but I play on. Soon there will be time for us to grieve, and for me to listen — really listen this time — to the stories of the home we may have lost forever. Soon there will be time to move back into my house. There will be time for school, guitar, Emily, and all of my friends. But for now, at this exact moment, we gather together, a family basking in the glow of my Dad's favorite song.

The song ends, and I can't help myself. I give a little flourish and add my own tune, the one I spent weeks fine-tuning. Raindrops fall from the top of the screen. Half become silver, the other half turn gold, but one turns a brilliant green, the same shade of green as the paint the kids dumped on me. The silver and gold raindrops drift to opposite ends of the screen, while the green one zips in, around, and among them, impossibly fast, becoming a blur, filling the screen.

I jump at a sound I've never heard before. Dad stands directly behind me. He's laughing. But he's also crying. In the projector's fading light, I see his face streaked with tears. He pulls me into an embrace that's as tight as the grip he held me in when he was trying to protect me from the Citadel's collapse. Dad presses his face into my hair and sobs. Then everyone else is there, wrapping their arms around us, gathering in close to reassure each other our home still exists.

See Michael Barron's story "River's Song" online at Metaphorosis.
If you liked it, leave a comment. Authors love that!
Remember to subscribe to our e-mail updates so you'll know when new stories are posted.

About the story

Honestly, I don't remember exactly when I got the idea for this story. The concept of an alien growing up on earth and thinking of herself as an earthling, even though her family has strong ties back to their home planet has been with me for a while. However, I didn't have anything specific in mind in terms of plot, conflict, character arches or characters in general so it just sat in the back of my mind for a while, occasionally rising to the surface when I was commuting to work or drying the dishes.

I didn't find anything to anchor this broad notion of a story until my wife and I went camping. I remember loading up the car and thinking about how it felt like our whole lives were in the back of my CRV. For some reason this made me think of this vague concept of a story, and I realized it was a moving story. My alien — later named River — has spent her whole life on earth but has been informed that they are moving to a home world she barely remembers. I figured the frame story would be River driving back to the place that will take her "home" and during the trip she would look back on her human life. The story didn't exactly turn out as I originally envisioned — seriously, when do they ever? — but finding this moving/road trip storyline gave me the direction I needed.

A question for the author

Q: What tools do you write with?

A: I do most of my writing early in the morning (it's not that unusual for me to wake up around 4:00). My typical writing setup is, a mug of black tea on my left, my long-haired orange cat (usually still asleep) on my right, my laptop on my lap, often with the lofi hip hop radio station playing in the background. Also, I need to acknowledge all the authors who have inspired my recent writing: T. Kingfisher, Becky Chambers, Stephen

Graham Jones, Chuck Wendig, as well as countless others who have been published in all the sci-fi / fantasy collections I have read.

About the author

Michael is the vice president of the North Baltimore Chapter of the Maryland Writers' Association. He is a member of the neurodivergent community, and his experiences inspire his writing. When he is not writing or reading, he is either training for a marathon with his wife or working as a librarian at the Baltimore County Public Library, where he teaches creative writing classes. He has also undertaken a never-ending quest to find the world's greatest hot sauce.

michaeljbarron.com, @Barron_Writer

Pain Eater

Danny Menter

Before the summer I turned twelve, plants had seemed innocuous: sometimes pretty, mostly boring, perennial background filler. I did know someone once who claimed her Ficus granted pleasant dreams when fed a mixture of honey and dried banana peel; another who swore his succulent had cannibalized his others while he was at work, leaving behind a massacre of black fertilizer and a noticeably plumper cactus sunning itself on the windowsill. But I heard those stories later, when I knew better, when I believed them.

It had always been there, thick and bulbous, rotating like a miniature planet in its harness, but I couldn't remember ever looking at it directly until that summer. I dropped the black plastic bags next to the toolshed, and pulled my grandfather's heavy work gloves off and left them on the wooden bench. Above, hung an assortment of rust spotted tools: hoes, trowels, and an axe with a heavy maple handle. I returned the shed key to its spot under the stone frog and turned back towards the plant.

I sifted through the sounds that had stopped me; beneath the soft tear of weeds ripping from the earth and sand shimmying into the trash bag, I thought I had heard a sigh, as if the giant thing had exhaled.

I looked back towards the house. Everyone had finished swimming and the grill crackled with burgers and hotdogs. The impromptu garden tidying had been Grandpa's idea, cut short by his dizzy spell—my enlistment in chores a frequent occurence while we lived with Grandpa and Grandma over the summer—now he sunned himself on the porch in a plastic Adirondack chair, a halo of pipe smoke hanging over his head. He looked faded, indistinct, a photo of a photo. Dad was setting up slender tubes on the concrete walkway, peering upward to ensure their trajectory.

I listened again, but the whole yard lay in a state of lazy, sunburnt silence—the only sound the creak of the chains bracing the plant as it rocked in the wind.

Later, Grandma took a thick bag of sugar out of the cupboard for shortbread.

"Twenty years or so?" She slid a tab of butter into the mixing bowl and leaned against the counter. She was short, only a head taller than me, in her red apron with multicolored fireworks threaded through the chest, but she had never seemed old, with her face like starched white linen. In the living room I could hear Dad talking about the progress on our new house, the one we would move into after the summer.

"Was it always that big?" I asked.

She glanced through the sliding glass door, but the afternoon sun obscured any view of the backyard.

"I wouldn't worry," she said, turning and dusting her hands on her apron, "your grandfather has always taken care of the weeds. I try not to pay attention to those things."

She handed me the mixing bowl. It was the size of my chest and I needed to sit down on the steps that led down into the sunken living room and brace it with my knees to maneuver the spoon.

Mom lay on the opposite couch, bathed in light, arm drifting across her forehead while Dad paced in the foyer making a sales call.

I grasped the spoon with both hands to work it around the bowl, but it barely budged. In a minute my forearms screamed, and Grandpa noticed and heaved himself from the recliner, squatted down next to me on the floor, and placed his callused hands around my small ones. Together we smoothed out the dough.

After dinner we filed out to the backyard. Beyond the stiff Saint Augustine grass, baked to glass by the heat, cut a chain link fence that separated my grandparents' yard from a retention ditch. Over the years, seeds and pollen drenched by rainwater and street runoff had erupted into a tangle of thorny vines and greasy flat-leafed vegetation that crowded at the fence, ready to tear it down if we let it. I stared at the boundary while

Dad lit the first of the rockets. It fizzled to life as Grandma handed us each a dense brick of shortbread from her cookie tin.

My eyes burned from an afternoon of swimming, but I forced them open against the sky to watch the rockets disintegrate into pink sparks.

A week later I sat on the concrete steps by the pool next to a crowded collection of aloe, spiny and prehistoric, and a skull of desiccated coral. I'd never worn a tie before. I kept clipping and unclipping it from my shirt collar.

Inside, mourners gathered, afraid to bump into each other, polite and fragile. Their whispering was too loud. A portrait of my grandfather, decked out in his navy uniform, sat on the kitchen table, encircled by a wreath of white lilies.

I wondered if I had a time bomb in my chest too, winding down to its final tic.

I loped out across the grass, the late afternoon sun an orange disk, to the plant.

It was so big it stretched against the chains suspending it from the oak, causing the tree to splinter along its trunk.

I placed my hand, pink from the heat, against the lime green skin of the thing. It was warmer than my hand, and something seemed to pulse beneath the surface. I imagined what it would be like to peel back all its layers, what it would hold in the center. An eye, maybe, bloodshot and swiveling, corded in inch-thick veins. Or nothing. Just more and more layers until you came out the other side.

Then I thought of snakes, and imagined one was hiding now, waiting for my hand to slide closer to one of the folds. I jerked away.

Dad joined me. He looked uncomfortable and sad, unsure of what to say.

"She'll be okay," he said finally.

"Who?" I asked.

"Well, both of them, I guess." He dug the heel of a black shoe into the earth. "But your mother," he added, before walking away.

I stared at the space next to the porch where a week before the five of us had watched stars explode in the sky.

A rustle and groan beside me, and I turned slowly towards the plant. I squinted, first with one eye, then the other.

I lifted my hand, measuring the distance between the plant and the pool door using my fingers.

I was sure.

It had grown.

On the kitchen table, Grandma's tin lay bare, its tarnished corners worn silver where the seams met. The last few guests edged out, sharing pained glances with me, offering to help with the bags of trash Dad held from his hand, his other on the door jamb.

I found it difficult to look anyone in the face. Mom and Dad and Grandma made movements that approximated normal, but were too fast and slow all at once, like the jerky movements of marionettes.

That night, Mom and Dad made a bed up for me in the living room, tucking a quilt into the couch cushions and draping it over me like an envelope. Grandma had gone to sleep, or at least retreated into a far dark corner of the house to be alone. I had never noticed how the house echoed when only one person was speaking, the sounds ricocheting off the walls like softballs.

I still felt that when I glanced at the recliner he'd be there, square jawed and immense, chewing the end of his pipe.

"Mom," I said, and the word felt funny, like I was saying it for the first time.

She waited in the doorway that led back to the bedrooms.

"That thing in the backyard—"

"Thing?" She said, closing her robe against her throat and bracing herself against the wall.

"The plant, I guess." Because maybe that's all it was.

"Oh, Bryan's plant." She read the silence, studied the room for a place to sit, but she seemed to see mines everywhere that could go off at the slightest pressure. Ultimately, she chose the step where I held the mixing bowl a week before.

"Bryan gave that to your grandmother a few weeks before the accident. A birthday gift." Her eyes creased at the corners. "You know, it was this big," she held her hands a few inches above one another, "when he bought it. He was always doing stuff like that. That's why he was the favorite."

Mom never spoke of her brother, who had died in an accident before I was born. I knew little about him other than that we shared a name.

I absorbed this, appreciating the way speaking helped fill up the room, and it felt clandestine, opening doors on the past that had been locked—peering into a time before I was born, a mythology I might never have access to again.

"Did you ever think about getting rid of it?" And I knew I'd made a mistake by the way her eyes froze, and her hand clawed its way back up her throat, as if someone had just thrown open the door on a blizzard and an icy wind was thrashing around the room. But the only change was my question, which had shorn the conversation in half.

"No, we couldn't." She stood, took a step forward, and flicked the light off.

Things were worse at the funeral. I was realizing that pain wasn't linear: it peaked and ebbed, then crested again unexpectantly, violently.

Mom had been quiet in the few days leading up to it. I watched her the way you watch tinder in a bonfire, wary and expectant. The funeral was held on the same grounds where Bryan was buried, Grandma told me. They even used the same priest, a tottering old man who asked me to hold the scripture readings for him at the lectern as he spoke. Everyone thought this was a great idea.

The same shopworn people who had come to my grandparents' home were there, milling around, checking their phones, keeping close to the perimeter.

Dad and Mom were fighting. Dad had to leave in the morning to catch a flight to Austin for a sales meeting, but Mom wanted him to stay to help Grandma pack up Grandpa's things. With the neighborhood getting more dangerous and Grandma alone, Mom thought it best to move her into a condo closer to our new house.

I could sense the hesitancy, a hole that suggestion had fallen into.

"Well, that may not be a good idea," Dad said.

"Why not? She could help with Bryan. and you said the house is nearly finished

anyway, we just need your final bonus to
—"

Dad rushed in "—I just don't think we should be too hasty, is all. With everything going on...the funeral, I mean... I... we may have to hold off on the move."

I could sense something change. A drop in pressure. A curdling of the air.

"We have savings for that, Dean." An electric current pulsed through each word.

They couldn't hear me on the outside of the door. I had come to tell them that I didn't want to hold the papers. I didn't want to stand in front of all those people in their caked-on suits and dresses, and not for the last time, I wished I had an older brother or sister to take my hand and tell me what to do. But instead, I wiped my face and forced the rock in my throat down to my belly, where it settled, and walked away. I imagined it growing in there, calcifying like the coral on Grandma's porch.

As I perched by the lectern, a man walked into the back of the parlor; I saw him over the greying heads, hunched slightly, wearing aviators and a creased leather jacket. Dad had his head bowed, but I could see him stiffen as he caught sight of him. The hymnal in his hands quaked. Mom turned too, but it was difficult to read her expressions, her emotions as opaque as sea-glass.

She placed a palm on Dad's and whispered something in his ear. He pushed her hands away to lie lonely and tangled in her lap.

"You have no right—" Dad was saying.

I froze in the doorway with a tray full of plastic wineglasses to throw away. Clearly a ploy to keep me from this scene.

The man in the leather jacket had one hand on a hip and the other outstretched, palm up, as if he expected Dad to shake it.

They were standing in the funeral parlor's kitchen area, forced close together by cardboard boxes filled with wine. I could smell aftershave that wasn't Dad's— something sickeningly spicy and sweet.

"It was in the paper. I just came to pay my respects," the man said. His accent was slightly southern, a cowboy in a Marlboro ad.

I felt hands on my shoulders moving me out of the doorway and back into the hallway.

Mom's face, close to mine: *Go,* she mouthed, but before I could retreat there was a massive crash and the shattering of glass, and the man stumbled out of the doorway pinching the bridge of his nose between his fingers. A crimson gush darkened the collar of his white shirt. He leaned his head back and disappeared wordlessly through a doorway to our right.

My hands were shaking, and plastic cups tilted off the tray, spilling their contents on the carpet. Dad came out next, massaging his knuckles, his face drawn and startled.

Mom stood with her hands on her hips. She glanced once through the doorway and her face collapsed, eyes jolting up at the corners, a choking sob breaking free of her lips.

Dad reached for her, but she turned away.

I got on my hands and knees, shaking, and began to stack the cups back on the tray. I held one up to the light. At the bottom, curled in a C, lay a slim finger of lime green vine.

The plant's sagging belly now dipped into the ground, making a little furrow of the muddy soil beneath. The top branches of the tree had begun to angle precipitously towards the roof of the house, and as I watched, a squirrel zigzagged across the shingles and clambered onto an outstretched limb. I was afraid to touch the plant—I could feel heat coming from it like a furnace. Whatever was inside was burning, fueling growth.

The man from the funeral, his nostrils stuffed with tissue, walked across the grass barefoot.

"Does Dad know he'll be here?" I had asked in the car ride over.

"He's an old friend; we need all the help we can get right now," she had said, not answering.

I eyed the plant and hoped it would shoot out leafy arms or vines and wrap him up like a mummy, twirl him up into pasta until the only thing visible was the top of his sweaty head, which would burst from the pressure, leaking red over green.

But I could sense that whatever the plant was, it wasn't benevolent; it merely squatted, motionless under its own gargantuan weight.

I stared down at the man's muddy feet, his jeans rolled over his bony ankles, and wondered what he had said to Dad in the funeral parlor. Dad, who didn't let me watch *Terminator* when it played on T.V.

"You know, I was there when he bought this—with your uncle, I mean." His voice twanged like a broken banjo string.

"Uncle Bryan?" I asked.

He squinted at it although storm clouds had covered the sun for hours.

"Yap. Knew your granda, way back when," he added.

"It looks like you know my dad, too," I said.

This stopped him and he looked at me for a moment, searching, then unconsciously reached for his nose but stopped himself and pointed at me instead.

"I think we maybe got off on the wrong foot yesterday. I'm Jake." He stuck out his hand and leaned over it like a magician coaxing a reluctant volunteer from a crowd.

It sank to his side when I didn't take it.

"I don't think I need to know your name," I said. "You're just here to help Mom. Then you're leaving."

His smile made my stomach turn acidic.

"Oh, I don't know," he said. "I might stick around for a while."

"Dad will be home tomorrow," I said, fast enough to run my words over one another.

He shook his head, mouth in a line but with a corner twisted up like a rusty hook.

"Nope. In Austin *all* week." He dragged it out in a way that made me aware of the sweat running down my back.

"Come look at this," Mom said. The three of them were hunched over a peeling leather photo album in the kitchen. I had been pacing the edge of the pool for an hour and I smelled like the outside that had seeped into my clothes.

I crossed my arms and edged forward reluctantly.

Jake had his hands on either side of the thing, as if he were holding the whole world of the album between his arms. Grandma and Mom were on either side of him. Grandma looked thinner, I realized, her parchment pale skin sagging at the corners of her mouth.

In the picture I saw Uncle Bryan, Mom's twin. He crouched next to a small motorcycle, hand placed on the shiny black seat. Behind him, I recognized Jake, although a much younger version, with long hair that swooped across his forehead. They were standing in the front yard, the oak trees smaller and the paint on the house a brighter shade of white. In the background, Mom rested her arms across a wrought iron gate.

There was no fence like there was now and I could see straight into the backyard where a small leafy plant dangled from a tree branch. It was light enough to suspend from a single nylon rope.

"He was so proud of that bike," Grandma said, turning from the table and busying herself in the kitchen.

"Is that..." I started, pointing at the bike.

Mom nodded, two fingers close to the edge of the photo, an inch or so away from Jake's.

"What happened to it?" I asked.

"After the accident, it wasn't nothing but scrap metal," Jake said. "I hauled it over to the junkyard."

Grandma made a pained sound in her throat and for a second I thought she had cut her hand, which grasped a potato, a paring knife in the other. Her head was tilted forward over the sink as if she was about to fall into it.

Jake scraped his chair away from the table and walked behind her, taking the blade. "Let me take care of this," he said. "Why don't you ladies take a load off and let the boys finish dinner?"

Mom gave him an appreciative glance that lingered in the air, then grabbed Grandma's arm and guided her into the living room.

"I need to shower," I protested.

"After dinner," Mom said. "Help Jake with whatever he needs."

Jake hauled a pot out of the cabinet under the sink and threw a washcloth over his shoulder. I was uncomfortable with the ease with which he knew the locations of items: the saltshaker, the grater, the ceramic butter plate. Things I never really paid attention to, but now felt imbued with importance; if I appreciated them more, he wouldn't have to touch them.

The light outside died as a fine drizzle greyed the yard. I heard the scrape of branches against the roof, their bent weight scratching like fingernails.

Jake stopped with a potato in one hand and stared intently at a picture above the sink. It was a photo of my mother when she was in high school, taken at prom or homecoming. In it, she perched on the edge of a couch, fingers laced under her chin, her head lifted towards the source of light shining from somewhere outside of the frame. Her hair had been curled, and it curved under her delicate chin in an auburn wave, the border of a pale green dress just visible at her collar. Mom usually never smiled in pictures, there were only a few I had seen where her teeth were visible, and because of this, I'd always liked this photo of her, imagining that this was who she was on some secret horizon. Her smiles were never given freely; they had to be earned, and anytime she did smile, I felt accomplished. I kept those moments close.

He leaned over the sink, and I tensed, watching his finger raise to stroke the frame.

"Don't," I said and felt my hands clench.

His head swiveled towards me, that grin leaking out of his face, running all over the place, spilling onto the counter.

"You know who took this picture?" he asked.

I don't want him to say it. There were fault lines running through this house and underneath were gaping mouths with sharp teeth and I wanted Dad to rush in and make him bleed again; it was a wash of rage and violence that I had never experienced before, and it tasted like terror.

He continued.

"Prom. I wore a blue tuxedo. Borrowed your uncle's bike—got home *real* late that night." He picked up the knife and potato and, in fine papery shavings, began removing the skin.

There was a shriek like two-by-fours being compressed by immense pressure. I heard a crack, too, but was unsure if it was the snap of wood or thunder.

He didn't look up as I snatched the phone off the receiver and darted into the hallway. Mom had taken to staying in Grandma's room, which left the only other bedroom open. I closed the door, locked it, and dialed Dad's number.

He picked up after what felt like too many rings.

"Everything okay?" he asked. I could hear traffic in the background, like he was at a street corner or a bus stop.

I tried to keep my voice level.

"When are you coming home?" I asked.

There was a long pause on the other end of the line.

"Well, it's taking a bit longer than I thought out here..." His voice trailed off.

"But we need...I think you should come home."

"Has something happened?"

Although I was thankful he had finally asked, the question lacked the urgency that I needed, and I had no idea how to answer.

"The plant—" I started, then thought better of it. What if it could hear me? What if even now there were tendrils snaking below the floorboards, finding cracks in the foundation, listening with a thousand different moist pores to this conversation. "I mean, Mom has the guy —"

A long sigh. Not the intake of breath, swear, yell, or shattering glass that I wanted from him.

"Jake," he said. "Your mother invited Jake over."

"Yes. I don't like him and he's saying things about Mom, and I think —" I was rushing through it and my thoughts were skittering like spiders but there was one thought that was coherent above all: "He should leave, Dad. I don't want him here."

"Listen," he said, "unfortunately, there's nothing that either of us can do about that right now. He's...kind of been in the picture for a while."

"But you...can't you just tell her she can't see him?" I said, and I felt tears breaking free and a hard knot forming in my throat.

"It's not that easy," he said. I heard voices in the background and laughing. "I just don't think your mother wants to hear from me right now."

I sensed finality; shovelfuls of dirt tumbling in over my head and light being shut out, closed coffins and stale air. I stared at the phone and ended the call.

I refused dinner, ignored Mom's voice when she called from the kitchen, then waited for a knock at the door, but none came. I crept silently into bed and listened to the probing life outside, trying to force its way in.

The next morning, I awoke to find Jake splayed across the couch, eyes lizard-like slits in the orange light spilling from the curtains. Mom walked in a moment later, saw me standing with my fists like rocks and Jake smiling slyly from the couch, but only gave herself a second to look guilty before she disappeared into the kitchen.

It took us three days get Grandpa's things packed up neatly into boxes and placed into the moving truck. Each box that was carted off felt like a little piece of my grandfather being cut out and tossed aside. I wanted to wrap my arms around everything in the house and keep it in place. I wanted to stop it all from slipping away. If enough pieces of him were gone then it was really happening, and there would be no going back. I wanted to tell Mom the secret that I knew: that we didn't have to go along with this; that death was just a rumor we didn't have to believe, and if we simply let it pass, he would come walking back in the door, Dad would return from his trip, Jake would fade away like a bad dream, and the plant would be destroyed forever.

Because that was the other thing I knew.

It was the plant that had started this, with its menacing leaves and the thing growing inside of it, and the vines which had now started to wind themselves underfoot, so that you had to watch them when you were carrying boxes across the thick grass. But every time I thought about damaging it—purposely running a dolly over a clammy limb or puncturing the swollen belly with a kitchen knife—Jake seemed to be there, watching.

"Your mother could use your help in the garage," Jake said, on the final day of packing, standing with his arms crossed and feet spread underneath the oak.

I trudged away, finding Mom paused at the brick wall of the garage, a plastic bag in her fist.

With her back turned I was able to stow the pocket-knife under a stack of wool quilts on a shelf where I had been hiding it. I needed something much bigger, I decided.

Mom didn't turn as I entered the garage. We hadn't spoken much in the last three days, not since I had foregone dinner the night after the funeral.

I watched her back now, thin under her t-shirt, all collarbones and elbows and long hair twisted up into a bun beginning to fray.

"Mom," I called.

She turned and her eyes, half-lidded, found mine. She was far away, and it took her a moment to swim back, whatever rip tide was pulling her away ebbing momentarily.

She gestured, and I grabbed the trash can and swung it over to her.

She tossed the bag in and settled heavily into a plastic lawn chair that lay in a triangle of light from the open garage door. Beyond, Grandma watched Jake rattle down the U-Haul's wide door.

At the end of the lawn, the retention ditch gave off a cloying smell, rotting vegetables and decay, and my stomach tensed.

"How did you ever live next door to that?" I said, wiping my mouth with a sleeve. "It reeks."

Mom glanced absently at the neon green wasteland beyond the chain-link fence and shrugged. "You can get used to anything."

I wanted to ask her so many things then: why they had kept the plant all these years, what had made it stop growing? If we escaped before awaking one morning to find it erupting in a slimy green spike from our mouths, would it simply follow us? Appear suddenly in the folds of a rose blossom, or wait as a seedling attached to an eyelash? Had we been spreading it this whole time?

But I settled on this: "What is Jake?"

She waved it away.

"He's an old friend, I told you that."

"More than that. He took you to prom. He was there when Bryan died. He was there when…"

She held a hand to her face, the flash of her wedding band floating through the garage like a lightning bug. She looked weak, fed upon. When she looked up again, her eyes moved past me.

Jake stood in the doorway, one hand holding the pocketknife. He tapped it against his thigh, slowly, then ushered me over. His eyes glinted. "Time for a talk."

I kept my distance from him as we circled into the backyard, through the faded wooden gate, under the smoldering afternoon sky, to stand again at the plant.

He picked his way across the grass, almost reverently, reaching out a hand but stopping short of touching the thing. His hand traced the veiny membranes like an ancient text he could read.

"Can you hear it?" he whispered.

Waves of disgust roiled through me at his proximity to the thing. Sweat beaded on his forehead. I wanted to run, but part of me needed to hear what he would say. Maybe there would be an answer, a clue, a way to kill it.

"It's special, you know." He shook his head, "Of course, we didn't know that when he bought it. It was just a green thing, a small fragile thing someone had left half alive in the back of a hardware store." He rubbed the damp area above his lip. "Your Uncle didn't want it, but I could sense it was..." he tossed his head, as if clearing it of fog.

Goosebumps rippled along the tops of my arms despite the heat.

"It spoke to me." His voice was toneless, eyes lost, and I took a step backwards. "It will give you what you want if you feed it. Anything you want." He angled his body towards the garage as if he could see through the brick and plaster to where Mom sat.

"No." I said, my voice a croak.

"We've been waiting," he droned, continuing. "I thought your uncle would be enough—"

The accident. Not an accident. Jake, who had used the bike before. Who had needed something, a sacrifice. Now, with Grandpa gone, the pain rippling through us had made it grow again. A cold, sick feeling flowed through me, and when I had the strength, I pried myself away from his dull, green gaze, and ran inside.

That night we ate a dinner of frozen pizza that tasted like used tea leaves. Jake never left Mom's side long enough for me to speak to her, so I retreated into the bedroom instead. I was lifting the window latch when Grandma tapped on the door and let herself in.

She carried something under her arm, a big book, leatherbound, that she set on the edge of the bed. "We haven't had the chance to talk," she said and pulled a wicker chair from the corner.

The book was filled with newspaper clippings, browned with age but preserved behind a yellowing sheet of plastic.

"You know your uncle passed away when he was young, only seventeen," she started.

"You don't have to do this," I said.

She glanced at me, watery blue eyes and papery skin, resting a small warm hand on my arm and smiled.

"You need to hear this, especially now," she said and began to flip through the album.

And she told me the story, of how bad it was, how Bryan took his bike out and they got the phone call an hour later and how they slept on the cold linoleum floor of the hospital for a week, waiting for him to wake up. How Jake had been there with Mom, and how, when something bad happens, the people who experience it with you, you never really forget, because the pain gets in under your skin and travels to your heart and if it wakes up again you go looking for those people who were with you before.

"The plant is going to keep growing," I whispered.

She closed the book filled with the images of Bryan.

"It may," she said.

"Aren't you scared?" I asked.

She nodded, put her hand underneath my chin.

And because I was eleven and because this wasn't even close to the answer that I needed, that I wanted, I waited until the house was asleep, and cracked the window, and slipped out into the rain.

The toolshed was a black mass with the bulky bags of yard waste that had never been thrown out still sitting next to the wall from weeks ago when I had watched those fires explode in the sky and Dad's hand was in Mom's and the pain was there, sure, but it was manageable, hadn't broken free from its constraints to destroy us.

My feet sucked at the muddy ground, each step filling with brown water, and my shirt was soaked by the when I reached the shed. The motion light flooded the yard with light, but it would be too late by the time they realized what I planned.

I scrabbled for the key underneath the stone frog and shoved open the doors. The axe, an old one, its blade nearly blunt but sharp enough, hung heavy from its peg. I needed both hands to lift it, and it banged into my shoulder painfully as I swung it down from the wall.

I dragged the axe behind me, tracing a line from shed to plant that created a little ditch of rainwater.

I heard shouting from the porch.

Lightning flashed and there was a shape in my path, arms outstretched to bar the way.

Jake. Who must have perched near the window all night, standing guard. His undershirt shriveled in the rain; dark hair plastered across his forehead.

He was a part of this thing, a parasite living on the fringes of pain, waiting for it to weaken its host before he consumed it. A slash of a smile sliced under his still swollen nose.

I didn't feel bad when the flat end of the axe smashed into his forearm, audibly snapping the bone like a piece of uncooked spaghetti.

He screamed and flung himself away from the next stroke, which whistled into the side of the plant with all my strength. For some reason I thought of my grandfather's hands on mine the night before he died, guiding me.

The axe sunk into the flesh with a wet *schlick.*

Suddenly, with a scream of wood rearranging itself, the oak straightened, tugging the chain upwards as putrid air and black liquid poured from the opening of the plant and hissed, steaming, onto the ground.

I heard Jake moaning to my right, propped against the screen of the porch and a cry from the patio as the sliding glass door shivered open and Mom and Grandma rushed out.

I was hacking frantically now, creating little triangles of green and yellow plant flesh. Piles of mushy vegetable matter rose at my feet, stinging my shins while my arms burned from the effort.

Soon the only thing left was a tiny, shriveled acorn; a wrinkled brown seed the size of my fist, connected to the chain which now swung freely in the wind.

I gathered the fallen pieces in my arms. They smelled like overripe bananas and the blankets of a person long sick. I stumbled under their weight and walked to the edge of the yard. There, I let the pieces slide from me, over the chain link fence and into the green waste beyond. I heard them rolling into the foliage on the far side, and the splash as they hit the water.

I collapsed into the mud. My shirt reeked of sweat and sickness and I pulled it off and threw it behind me over the fence.

The floodlamp illuminated the place where the plant hung. Mom recoiled from Jake, the spell broken somehow, as he grasped at her with his one good arm. He appeared small, depleted. Grandma moved through the rain, the light framing a face shrouded in shadow. She approached, feet squelching through the mud.

I expected to see her smile, but when the lightning cracked again her face looked worn, carved from marble, eyes drooping at the edges in sorrow.

"It's okay," I splayed my fingers out against the light from the porch so I could see her face better, maybe her expression was simply a trick of the light. "I killed it."

But she shook her head.

"Don't you think we've tried?" she answered softly.

And I felt then the press of growing things at my back, an entire ditch filled and probing at the edges, a lifetime of pain hacked and discarded, yet continuing to grow. What grandfather had tended, what his death had unleashed.

I saw the heart of the thing, swaying gently from the chain, a single, fragile leaf breaking free.

I pulled on the gloves, too big for my hands, and grabbed a roll of black trash bags. The morning had dawned bright and brutal, the air thick, and Grandma brought me ginger ale while I worked, removing patches of rotting rosebushes, digging up rectangles of brown grass, and heaving husks of the plant into a lined trashcan.

She handed me the sweating glass and I pressed it against my forehead, the sensation painfully refreshing in the heat.

Mom had entered the bedroom at dawn while I pretended to sleep, and curled her fingers through my hair, kissing my forehead.

"He's gone," she whispered, then, before she left: "Dad will be home tomorrow."

Jake had disappeared after I had attacked the plant, evaporating into the rain-soaked night without a word. I hadn't decided whether to tell Mom of Bryan's accident, whether I thought it *was* an accident. But for now, it was enough that Jake was gone.

Grandma and I lingered in the yard, watching the stunted plant quiver slightly, but hold its shape.

I thought of all the times Grandpa must have fought the grief that threatened to destroy him. How many times he must have pulled on these same gloves and hacked away at the plant, knowing it would just grow back, sometimes quickly, sometimes slowly.

"There isn't a way to destroy it, not really, it'll just spread," I said to her. She patted my hand silently and made to walk back across the grass to the porch, then turned, looking up at the wide oak trees, the flowers blazing along the paving stones in hues violet and cream, until her gaze settled on me.

And she smiled, adding: "But we can let it starve."

See Danny Menter's story "Pain Eater" online at Metaphorosis.
If you liked it, leave a comment. Authors love that!

Remember to subscribe to our e-mail updates so you'll know when new stories are posted.

About the story

Growing up in Central Florida, my grandparents had this massive Staghorn Fern hanging from an oak tree in their backyard. If you've never seen one, look one up. They're these kind of odd, layered, bulbous leafy balls that grow and grow and grow—they had this particular one for almost thirty years. It always seemed vaguely ominous to me, probably due to its immense size, and it hung right outside their screened in porch so when you were swimming, or really doing anything in the backyard, it was always on the periphery, watching. So, it was easy to turn it into the source of evil in the story. The rest of the narrative is constructed from events that happened to me when I was a kid: my parents split up shortly after the passing of my grandfather, and my mother remarried soon after. Far scarier than anything else when you're young is to have your stability threatened. As an adult, you have a longer view of how events will play out, but as a kid you really have no idea what's going to happen next. Later, it became more apparent why my grandfather's passing had such an effect on the family dynamic, opening wounds that hadn't ever healed.

I initially wrote this as a journal assignment for a course on magical realism, and the horror/supernatural aspects of the plot were more understated, partially to emphasize that the narrator, an eleven-year-old, seems to be the only one aware of the danger his family is in. I wanted to put the spotlight on the different ways people deal with trauma, through avoidance, acceptance, or anger—and underline how when you're a kid, or at least, when I was a kid, you sometimes want something as simple as a monster to sink an ax into to put everything back together.

A question for the author

Q: Are you an outline or discovery writer?

A: A little bit of both, to be honest. I generally start with an image or scene, then work outwards from there. I'll have a general idea of where the story is headed based on the characters, and plot, but I almost never outline specific scenes. Most of the fine tuning comes later, when I see the fleshing out that characters need, or if there are any glaring plot holes. Especially in a first draft, I like to see where the story wants to go on its own with as little guidance from me as possible, although lately I've been playing with prompts and other constraints as a way to prime the engine. Being able to bounce ideas off some kind of boundary, whether that be a word limit, plot detail, or form, can be a lot of fun.

About the author

Danny Menter grew up in Central Florida, fled to Madrid after graduating from Florida State University, and currently lives outside of Chicago, Illinois. He is a teacher by day, and is currently pursuing a Master of Fine Arts in Fiction.

@MenterDanny

The Zoo Diaries

Frances Pauli

Part Three

Previously…

At the Rainriver Zoological Gardens, one escape became the catalyst for a series of unfortunate incidents. The tortoise, Oliver, roamed the zoo as a fugitive, searching for his missing cage mate. When the Zoo-cam caught him interacting with the elephant, Shanti, zoo attendance spiked, putting more pressure on the animals inside and increasing crowd-related stress. The lion, Charlie, got his first whiff of hotdog when the bustling crowd began dropping things into his enclosure. The macaque, Gonzo, assuaged his caffeine addiction with a stolen latte, and Oliver, intent on continuing his search, enlisted the dubious aid of one of the zoo's resident pigeons. Together, they searched for the aviary, to find the missing crane, Miranda. Pleased with the increased revenue, the zoo announced the first ever photo and video contest.

Tortoise Abroad

Oliver will spend the day in a playground. The pigeon leads him there, shows him a concrete tunnel made to resemble a prairie dog colony. She talks non-stop, but Oliver has grown accustomed to her prattle, grateful for the bird's guidance.

Her voice is nothing like Miranda's, but it is a bird voice. It soothes him. He remembers long days conversing with his love while she stalked through the reeds or fished for the dead minnows sprinkled across the shallow pond.

Oliver ducked into the pseudo-burrow at dawn, and he spends the day missing Miranda, remembering her high voice, and wondering if the pigeon will return when night falls again.

She has fluttered off in pursuit of crumbs, which she insists are more plentiful around the playground where he's hidden.

During the day, children swarm the equipment. Many find Oliver, snug in the depths of their territory. He endures their rattling pats, and when he tires and tucks his head inside his shell, the pounding of small fists against his carapace.

They squeal and giggle, but he is unharmed, armored against their attention.

For a while he fears they will reveal him to They-who-keep-the-fences-barred, but their pronouncements that, "a turtle is in there," are inevitably met with disdain.

"That's nice, dear." Or "Whatever you say, honey."

Oliver waits, patient as the concrete around him. When the burrow mouths grow dark, he creeps to one end and finds the pigeon waiting.

"You're back," he says.

"The aviary is just across the way." She hops in place, flaps as if contemplating alighting on his shell again.

"Show me." Oliver heaves himself into the open.

"It's that building right over there." The pigeon bounces into the air, flies less than three strides before landing again. "Come on."

Oliver hurries his feet. He's been close, right across from the aviary all day long. Miranda waits for him, and he churns his stump legs and follows the pigeon with all his fervor renewed.

The warm nap in a concrete tube may have helped.

Oliver feels his goal now, just past the edge of his plastron. He runs for it, in as much as a tortoise *can* run, and only when he stands in its shadow does his next problem become apparent.

"How do I get inside?" he asks.

"Through the double doors," the pigeon coos. "You'll have to wait for someone to open them."

"If they see me," Oliver moans, "they'll catch me, put me back where I started."

"It's the only way in," the bird insists. But she follows Oliver, just the same, when he makes a ponderous circuit around the building, a fortress, it turns out, accessible only through that trap of twin doorways.

To her credit, she does not rub it in when he resigns himself.

"It's the only way in," he says.

The pigeon only puffs slightly and bobs agreement.

Pigeon

Peg convinces the tortoise to risk everything. He is desperate and carries opportunity in his massive domed shell.

They wait together through the long night. At times, he dozes. At times, he paces the aviary perimeter. Peg naps atop his shell. She dreams of a jungle where there is no battle with crows. No struggling over cast-off scraps.

When the first sunlight makes their position too conspicuous, she drives her partner to a nearby bush to hide while They-who-cage-animals go about their morning duties.

Oliver is restless, anxious. He shifts but doesn't bolt. Not even when two of the staff briefly open the double doors.

"Wait," Peg coos. "It has to be the guests."

They-who-cage-animals are far too cautious. They never open both sets of doors at once.

Oliver stirs but does not step. He breathes loud enough to reach her but does not speak. The time comes when They-who-cage-animals move on, and the great gates are opened at last.

Peg shifts her weight from one clawed foot to the other. She watches the tide of visitors wash down the paths, and she whispers to Oliver, "Wait. Wait."

The visitors lap up against the aviary entrance. They abandon their strollers, lift squirming children into their arms and begin the jostling dance that will lead them, a few at a time, through the double set of doors.

"Now," Peg hops, forgets her perch is mobile, and nearly topples to the path when Oliver lurches forward.

He is too massive. Peg realizes this as they rock and stumble toward a moving wall of legs, a multi-hued barrier of trousers, sandals, skirts, and sneakers. The crowd is thicker than she expects.

But Oliver is determined. He is more agile than Peg believes, and the crowd is far less observant than she fears. It is going to work.

The tortoise ducks into the press, and the legs adjust, work their way to either side like a stream parting for a rock in its middle.

They are slow, but they are moving. Peg has to hunker, to cling and lower for fear of being knocked aside. The doors open, close, open. Each time too brief, too short to risk invasion.

Until Oliver wedges himself into the gap.

Someone presses the glass against his side, squeezes, and when he doesn't give, bangs the panel hard against his shell before noticing why it will not close. Voices brattle nonsense above, loud, barking sounds that do not move the obstacle.

The door is ajar. Oliver heaves his body into the space between the outer and inner portals.

Peg flaps, makes ready.

The crowd is wary today. They read the signs. The outer portal closes, shuts in a tortoise and a bird, trapping them. Peg tenses, steadies.

Someone inside the aviary wants to leave. They do not look first, do not care about signs. The inner door opens and Peg launches. She flutters inside, flapping her wings as whoever opened the door ducks and squeals. Peg flies over their head, flies into warm, wet air and the constant singing of other birds.

She has made it. She is in.

She flaps to a high window, perches in a slash of light above the fronds, and surveys paradise.

Far below, the struggle to dislodge a tortoise from the space between doors continues. The crowd is divided, in or out, and Peg does not see what decision is made. She does not care.

She has attained her goal, and pigeons are only concerned with their own happiness.

The Crow

Debra watches as the tortoise is recaptured. She has come to the aviary in search of gossip, but she finds her murder hovering at the roof's edge. When she shoves her way into the line of crows, there is a ripple effect. The line bounces and grumbles, but all eyes remain down, fixed on the doors below.

There, a huddle of keepers has formed. They have cleared the area of guests and strollers, and a few break from the herd, stand back, and keep the crowd on the paths moving along to other exhibits.

The outer doors are propped open, held wide by a garbage bin and a wedged stone. Several keepers bend over, half in and half out of the space. They work at something, raise and shift and bend their knees under the weight of their cargo.

Debra hops and opens her beak but does not caw. The moment is too heavy, too perfectly dire to break the silence.

She sees them drag the tortoise from the vestibule. She sees his feet thrashing at empty air as the keepers manage to get him off the ground.

They set him down outside and, carelessly, release their grip on his shell. Immediately, he charges the doors again. They dive, struggle to drag him back while one of the open-sided zoo vehicles beeps its way through the crowd in the aviary's direction.

Debra sees them load Oliver into its short bed. They climb in beside him while the crowd cheers. The clapping thunders, not nearly as satisfying as the report of a rifle. Still, the wanderer is caught fast. He has failed, and the crows celebrate by joining their voices to the cacophony.

Debra caws with them, cries until she is hoarse. But there is something wrong, too. Something she can't quite name. Something that feels like a shadow draped over them all.

In the truck, the tortoise struggles, spins and lifts and nearly topples himself. He has tasted freedom, perhaps. He has found something that teaches him how to fight.

She knows he will be jailed again. He will not be shot, perhaps, but his freedom was always a ruse. Still, as the vehicle pulls away, she does not follow. Something is wrong.

In her dark belly, a new thing is born. It twists, and nibbles, and feels far too much like envy to be taken seriously.

Ape House

Gonzo is outside when they return with Oliver. His troop has gathered near the bars, where the crowd sneaks them peanuts purchased from the elephant station. There are signs that forbid this, but the tide of visitors is too plentiful, out of hand, and obsessed with capturing their contest videos.

In order to watch the tortoise enclosure, Gonzo has to climb the ropes. He swings up, onto a high 'vine' in order to see over the many heads, the faces that always, inevitably, show too much tooth.

It irritates him to look at them, like a biting insect caught beneath his pelt. High in the ropes, however, he can breathe again, unclench his paws.

The tortoise is unloaded from the rear of a zoo vehicle. He is placed on a tarp that has been spread across the pathway, and They-who-keep-fences-barred lift the fabric on all sides. They raise the stout animal and carry him to his concrete wall, resting him on its top for a breath. Oliver teeters, swings his legs ineffectively. Then, with a final, coordinated, effort, he is wrangled inside again.

They settle him against his grassland, unwrap and free him with a great round of self-congratulation and cheering.

Gonzo presses his face into the bars. He clutches them at either side of his head. He watches, as Oliver drives a steady, straight path toward his open burrow. He means to leave again. Gonzo knows this in his gut, a warm certainty. The tortoise is not deterred by the futility of his effort.

Something has changed. It feels like more has gone wrong than just one tortoise outside his enclosure. An expectation hangs over the zoo now. A certainty that something else is about to happen.

And even though Gonzo is sure They-who-keep have filled in the long avenue of escape, he believes the tortoise will dig again. He will never stop digging.

Gonzo screeches encouragement. He bares his teeth and bounces on the rope. Dig! His heart chants it. Dig, friend. Dig for us all.

Gonzo sags against the bars. He screeches silently, a defiant stretching of lips. His nostrils widen, and he catches his bean again. It is everywhere in the crowd, as prevalent as the clicking cameras.

Today, Gonzo sees a paper vessel in each free, hairless paw. He sees them dancing just beyond the bars. It is forbidden to reach through. There are fences to keep the visitors back, stones and hoses to punish a monkey's bravery.

But today, the crowd ignores the signs. Today, the eager videographers lean close, shove, and shuffle, and even step briefly over the fence.

Gonzo leaps to the next vine. He hoots and swings, showboating for the crowd as he never does. He becomes a trooping monkey, a clown.

The cameras surge forward. They click like a hissing storm, but they bring the vessels with them. Gonzo watches. He is fast. He is cunning. When his paw strikes out, it is true. It is sure as the stones that will be thrown at him.

He snatches the vessel and snaps back, nearly losing it at the bars. His paws cradle, steady. He backs away with the treasure and is already bringing it to his lips. He drinks, and his body shudders, releases an orgasmic tension. It is worth the stones. It is worth everything.

Dig, my friend.

He guzzles the bean, shaking, trembling with relief and fear at his own brazen actions.

Then, inexplicably, the crowd begins to cheer. The teeth gleam around him, but no stones assault his hide.

They-who-gape clap, cheering for the macaque with his stolen latte. They sing to him, taking their pictures while Gonzo drinks.

ZOO

The contest website fills with videos. Someone's nephew, now promoted to webmaster, works full-time to keep the servers from crashing. There are 28 pages in the still photo gallery, and since he has allowed direct uploading, he is kept busy weeding out the irrelevant and the intentionally inappropriate.

When Gonzo's latte video hits the stream, it leaps to the top of the lists. The hearts fly as viewers show their appreciation for 'a good cup of jo'.

Commenters commiserate. Self-appointed internet police warn of the dangers of caffeine. One plucky student posts a history of macaques and coffee plantations.

Debate rages.

For a total of ninety minutes, Gonzo's latte escapade is the center of the zoo world's discourse. When someone posts, 'lion kisses little boy', however, the hearts move along. The list shuffles. An addicted macaque pales beside the unfettered adorableness of Charlie attempting to eat his tiniest visitor.

The world watches, swooning as the boy squeals in delight, as the lion's mouth stretches, and the enormous pink tongue washes a pane of clear, unbreakable glass.

Zoo attendance skyrockets.

The visitors become unruly, and the Board is forced to hire security.

Elephant Paddock

Shanti plants herself over Oliver's tunnel. Her four, tree-trunk legs cage in the irregularity in her paddock's terrain.

She stands guard, and she counts the zebras as they circle. They trot in a frantic huddle around their perimeter while They-who-keep-fences backfill Oliver's other hole. The equines are more flighty than usual, driven to constant panic by the growing crowds.

Shanti has dragged some hay out of her shelter. She tosses it over her broad back, a sign of her own nervousness. There are six digging. Three shovels and twelve boots that stamp down what the shovels throw into the opening.

She imagines Oliver will dig again. Though she spent little time with him, her impression has quickly cemented. He is stalwart, determined. Shanti wants him to win.

If she hides this exit, perhaps he will not have to dig so far. Perhaps, she will ensure that his flat face emerges in the right place. In the place where she can count him again.

They-who-fill-holes throw their dirt, stomp their boots into the earth. Shanti thinks they are not smarter than her tortoise. She thinks they will lose, and she stands guard over her secret, a massive gray sentinel waiting for the next escape.

Hyena Removed

Eventually, Alice speaks to the cat. She resists the urge until the boredom becomes unbearable, but this is not really as long as she'd intended. Creeping close to the front bars, she presses her nose into the aisle and whimpers.

"Your noise is irritating," the cat says. "Your face is unpleasant."

"Is not," Alice whines. "It is *my* face."

She remembers that the cat has told her this before, that she does not care for him, that he is mean and that he likes to lounge on his own shelf in silence.

But she is also lonely. She is afraid of this new-old cage.

"My cubs are missing," she says. "And you are an *unpleasant* cat."

"Sold." The cat pads to his cage front and gazes out at her.

Perhaps he is bored and hunting for sport. Perhaps, he is simply a foul-spirited animal. Alice believes she is an easy target either way. She is lost, and the cat has all the power.

"When cubs are big enough." He purrs and rubs against the bars. "They are sold to other zoos."

"Why?" Alice sits, panting, flicking her ears as if to dodge the cat's words. The horrifying concept. She is, despite her ignorance of the fact, a family sort of animal, and this idea of selling cubs disturbs her.

"Why not?" the cat tosses back. "My cage is too small to share. My belly is too hungry. If my get scatters to the corners of the world, it is only fitting. It is only the way of things."

"For cats, maybe," Alice says. "Cats have cold hearts."

She snaps her heavy jaws, snaps at the cat and the idea of her cubs, lost, sent to other zoos with no matriarch to learn from. Alice remembers that she does not like cats. That this one, in particular, is vile.

"Sultan," she snarls. "Your name is Sultan."

"What of it?" He shrugs with his whole body. "What of cubs and hearts? There is no room in your cage for others, beast. There is no room in any of our cages. Why should we pine for what we cannot keep?"

Alice gives him her teeth. She would teach him a lesson if there were no bars. She would show him how *unpleasant* she can be. But there *are* bars. There is an aisle and a narrow ledge and three dark walls with no view.

Alice groans and shakes herself. She rises, pads to the rear of the cage where she can face a corner and pretend there is no Sultan.

This is not her cage. This is not her life. She has no choice but to wait until it is over.

Lion Enclosure

Charlie dreams of the veldt. His legs twitch against the straw in his den. His whiskers tighten, pulling his face into a grimace. He dreams while the sky is dark, and the zoo is quiet.

The veldt smells of meat. Dry winds wash the scent over the long grasses. They carry the heat and the aroma to a stand of anorexic trees where the lions wait, lounging in the shade.

Charlie has never seen a veldt, but this dream comes from a place of memory and instinct, a generational place that is absolutely certain of the grass and the trees. He knows as well that the biting insects are legitimate. Their little stings make his hide shiver, and their noise is a rushing buzz in his velvet ears.

The scent, too, feels authentic, though he is troubled by the detail of it. Something about the aroma feels out of place, artificial. His brain has substituted the squeaky meat, superimposing the experience of a waking zoo on the sleeping lion.

Charlie opens his jaws and huffs. His tail lashes against dust and smashed down grass.

In the distance, an animal screams. Charlie's belly rumbles. The lions around him are unfamiliar, unfocused shadows beneath the trees. The dream blurs them, but out across the grass, Charlie's vision crystallizes. He sees as clearly as if he were mere inches from the far-off scene.

A struggling beast thrashes on one side. Its hooves paw in the air as death spasms through its tawny body. Charlie is far away, but the dream shows him the gleaming of each hoof, the splatter of blood across a heaving flank, and the patterned swirl of individual hairs.

He salivates. He huffs and lets his sides heave with it. Beside their prey, two lionesses move, pale death in paler grass.

Their jaws clamp around the beast's throat. They lift the front of it, drag it toward the pride beneath the trees.

Charlie's belly growls again. Drool pools at the corners of his muzzle. He watches them come, carrying the limp gazelle one step at a time. He watches, and just when they drop the carcass on the ground before him, he wakes up.

Grizzly Grotto

Hector's hip pinches when he tries to sit. He wakes late, and when his paws push against the den flooring, little pains dance through his wrists and neck.

He thinks he is an old bear.

He thinks it has been many years since he was fed from a bottle by Those-who-give-care.

He will miss the artist at this rate.

Wincing, showing his enormous teeth to the bare den walls, he forces his heavy, complaining body to rise. His ears lie flat against his skull. His black lips ripple, but he rubs his paws over his face and works out the little agonies with a slow undulation of his spine.

Some days are worse than others, but Hector remembers a time when he awoke with no pain, no stiffness in his bones at all.

The square door to his den has already been opened. The light sliding in through that gap is too bright. He has lingered over his dreams, played with his brother again, and the morning has run on without him.

Hector thinks of the artist and shoves himself to all fours. He limps only a few steps before the needle pains dim. By the time he trundles through the doorway, he feels like himself again. He is bear, king of his domain.

Warm sunlight against his fur erases the last of his stiffness. He lumbers, his body rolling with each step.

Beside his stump, there is a pile of chopped fruit, a few heads of wilted cabbage, and a miraculous sliver of honeycomb. Hector's mouth waters, but he looks to the railing first. He gazes up, beyond the trench, to the place where the artist stands.

She has waited. Her paws wave to him.

Hector adjusts his gait, smooths his steps, and walks with dignity to the offering of sweet food. Only when he tries to sit again does the sharp pain return. His hip twinges, and instead of the graceful pose he intended, he flops into a half-lounge on one side.

Hector pretends it was intentional. He yawns to show how little he cares and reaches with one paw for the waxy honeycomb. His arm seizes. Hector roars against a shooting pain, lets the sound out before he can catch it. He falls to his side, curls around his shoulder and roars again. All thought of his dignity fades in the black wave that is his bones complaining.

Dimly, he hears the voices above, the crowd at the railing calling to one another. He thinks of the artist only for a single, dark breath, but he is too weak to focus. Too busy trying to find a position that does not hurt him.

He lies still, breathes for ages, waits until his body releases him, and then remains on his side a good while longer.

By the time he can sit, the artist is no longer at the railing. They-who-keep-cages-locked have joined the crowd. Everyone stares into Hector's enclosure, witnessing, gaping, and not even taking a picture.

Tortoise Enclosure

Oliver drags the soft dirt from his tunnel, packing it carefully to the sides or pulling it, step by step, to a branching passage he no longer has need of. He works for three nights straight before he reaches the place where he changed direction, diverting from the zebra enclosure to Shanti's paddock.

The latter path stands open, has not been obstructed by They-who-keep-fences-locked.

Oliver sits in this junction and blinks, for long moments, in the face of his good fortune. It has not occurred to him that he might find any portion of his escape route overlooked, and the free pathway takes on an insidious aura.

He has heard about traps. He has recently re-learned this lesson. Thoughts of his recapture drive his head back inside his shell. He reconsiders the elephant tunnel, gauges how much night remains, and makes the conservative decision to wait for another day.

When his back faces that open exit, Oliver relaxes. He retraces his digging journey back to his own pen and emerges into inky night.

"There he is," a voice above his head calls.

"There. There he is."

Oliver hears that they are pigeon voices. He cringes, even before a rain of fat, feathered bodies land on the ground around his burrow mouth.

"Go away," he snaps.

The pigeons shuffle, feathers brushing one another in the darkness. The birds bob and weave. They are shadows dancing, and Oliver has had enough of their kind.

"We want in," one announces.

"It's not fair," says another.

"Leave me alone." Oliver moans and pushes himself onto the cropped grass. "No more pigeons."

"We'll take you to the aviary," one voice coos.

"We'll find your friend," another picks up the refrain.

"We want in."

Oliver lunges for the latest speaker. The pigeon squawks and flaps into the air. Oliver turns slowly, but his neck is long and flexible. He stretches, waves his head at one after another of the birds until they give up and move to the fence where he cannot reach them.

"It's not fair," they chant. "We want in."

"There's no way in," Oliver moans, gives in at last to his despair, and lets his limbs sag. What does it matter if the way is clear? There is no path into the aviary, at least not for a tortoise. His plastron rests on the cool grass, and he fights off a sob. "I can't get inside the aviary."

The pigeons coo and strut. They are not convinced. But it is a different voice that calls out next, a dreadful, scratching voice in the darkness.

"She's not in the aviary," the crow says. "She never was."

"Who, who, who," the pigeons echo one another.

"His bird friend," the crow answers. She hops from the shadow of the macaque's cage and bounces over Oliver's fence. "She's in the marshland, under the big nets."

"Nets?" Oliver speaks, even though he knows the crow is made of lies. Even though, like all the animals she taunts, he hates her. "What nets?"

Debra tilts her head to one side, mantles her black wings, and lets her tail feathers open and close before answering. She is dragging it out, baiting him.

Oliver knows this, too.

When she makes her answer, however, he has already decided to trust her.

"I can show you," Debra caws. "I can take you to her."

The pigeons protest. They explode into a frenzy of bobbing, of hopping in place and puffing out their feathers. Oliver ignores them. He has heard about traps. He has learned. But he thinks he is wiser than the crow. He thinks he can out-play the bird's game.

He thinks he may as well find out.

"Tomorrow night," he says.

And the crow makes no answer.

Ape House

Gonzo watches They-who-bring-food as they move between cages, but today they have left their vessels in the center of the aisle. When they bring fruit and biscuits to the macaque enclosure, Gonzo joins the others at the tub. There is no point in sulking, no hope of a stolen beverage this morning.

He has already enjoyed his moment of victory, and at least his headache has subsided.

Gonzo sucks on a dry biscuit. The latte's effects have faded, but he can still taste it if he concentrates. He feels calmer, less irritable. When the troop members tumble into him, he is less likely to bite or scratch them.

He feels better than he has in all his time at the zoo, and his quick brain already wonders if he can risk another vessel grab. To his surprise, he has not been punished. No stones were thrown, and the crowd from which he snatched the drink showed only pleasure at his daring.

They cheered for him, and Gonzo wonders if they may have been testing his boldness all along. He wonders if they didn't *want* him to steal the bean for himself.

He chews his biscuit, turning it over in his paws and tasting each side. The troop works its way through the fruit, then tires and begins its exodus out the little square door.

Gonzo decides to join them. He imagines a crowd gathered, a dozen fists clenched around paper cups. He chews his biscuit faster and even takes a sideways, shuffling step toward the exit before a strange noise stops him.

He turns back to the bars.

He-who-sweeps is standing very close to the cage. When Gonzo looks, he purses his pink lips and makes the noise again, a slurping, smooching sound that is accompanied by a gesture with both paws. They tap against the ledge outside the bars.

Gonzo screeches. He shows his long teeth.

He-who-sweeps looks over his shoulders, looks left and right, and then taps again. He smells nervous, twitches and smooches again.

When Gonzo bares his teeth and lunges, He-who-sweeps backs away from the cage. He collects his broom and rubs it across the aisle, but his eyes are still on Gonzo. He is waiting.

Gonzo sniffs in disgust. The act brings a strange scent to his nostrils, an aroma from just beyond his bars. It is both sweet and bitter. It is bean, but it is also something else, something new.

He cannot see a vessel, but his bean is there. He-who-sweeps has brought it. Gonzo shuffles to the bars and eyes the ledge. He pulls back his lips and inhales.

Three tiny coffee cherries wait just outside the bars. They are neither plump nor red, but they shine in the same familiar fashion. Their black surface makes a smooth skin, and Gonzo can smell the bean inside it.

His paws reach through. His eyes flick to the aisle and back.

He-who-sweeps watches as Gonzo snags the offering. He shows his teeth as the macaque places a cherry between his lips.

Gonzo cringes, uses his tongue to work at the sweet-bitter coating that, it turns out, is not a cherry skin at all. He sucks at it, finds it pleasant enough. When he reaches the core, however, Gonzo bites. He chews the bean, crunches it in his teeth and feels the rush of pleasure.

It is strong, smoky, and not green at all, but the act of chewing soothes him in a way the paper drink could not. Gonzo chews all three, bouncing from one foot to the other. He chews in ecstasy, in memory of a far-off jungle. He rolls the dry bean bits over his tongue, dribbling from the corner of his mouth. He holds it, holds it until the urge to spit is too strong.

Only when he gives into that urge at last, does he remember He-who-sweeps. His eyes focus, fly to the aisle where the other primate waits. Holding his broom still, showing his teeth, and bouncing, as Gonzo bounced, gleefully from one foot to the other.

See Parts I, II, and III of Frances Pauli's story "The Zoo Diaries" online at Metaphorosis.
If you liked them, leave a comment.
Authors love that!
Remember to subscribe to our e-mail updates so you'll know when new stories are posted.

Copyright

Title information

Metaphorosis March 2023

ISSN: 2573-136X (online)
ISBN: 978-1-64076-253-4 (e-book)
ISBN: 978-1-64076-254-1 (paperback)

Copyright

Metaphorosis Magazine is an imprint of
Metaphorosis Publishing
Neskowin, OR, USA

www.metaphorosis.com

"Metaphorosis" is a registered trademark.

Discounts available

Substantial discounts are available for educational institutions, including writing workshops. Discounts are also available for quantity purchases. For details, contact Metaphorosis at metaphorosis.com/about

Metaphorosis Publishing

Metaphorosis offers beautifully written science fiction and fantasy. Our imprints include:

Metaphorosis Magazine
Plant Based Press
Verdage
Vestige

You can also find us:
@MetaphorosisMag, @Metaphorosis
www.facebook.com/metaphorosis

Help keep Metaphorosis running by supporting us at
Patreon.com/metaphorosis

See more about some of our books on the following pages.

Metaphorosis Magazine

Metaphorosis

a magazine of speculative fiction

Metaphorosis is an online speculative fiction magazine dedicated to quality writing. We publish an original story every week, along with author bios, interviews, and notes on story origins.

We also publish monthly print and e-book issues, as well as yearly Best of and Complete anthologies.

Come and see us online at magazine.Metaphorosis.com.

Metaphorosis
Best of 2016
Metaphorosis
2016
Editor
B. Morris Allen

Plant Based Press

Vegan-friendly science fiction and fantasy, including anthologies of the year's best SFF stories, from 2016-2020.

Chambers of the Heart
speculative stories
by
B. Morris Allen

A heart that's a building, a dog that's a program, a woman sinking irretrievably — stories about love, loss, and motion.

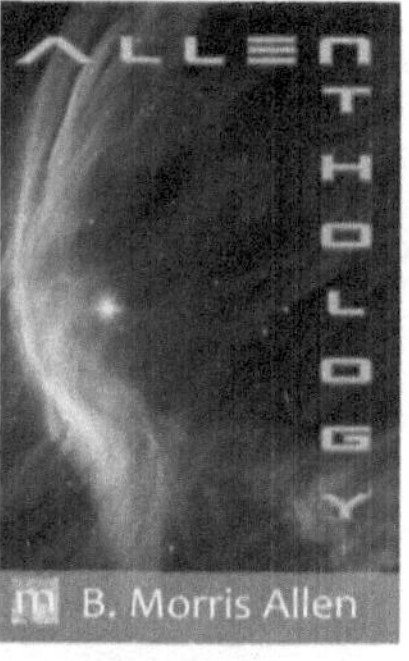

Susurrus

A darkly romantic story of magic, love, and suffering.

Allenthology: Volume I

Including three full collections of SFF stories.

Verdage

Science fiction and fantasy books for writers — full of great stories, often with an additional focus on the craft of speculative fiction writing.

Reading 5X5 x3

Changes

How do stories move from 'maybe' to published?

Here are 15 case studies of stories published in *Metaphorosis* magazine.

Reading 5X5 x2

Duets

How do authors' voices change when they collaborate?

A round-robin of five talented science fiction and fantasy authors collaborating with each other and writing solo.

Including stories by Evan Marcroft, David Gallay, J. Tynan Burke, L'Erin Ogle, and Douglas Anstruther.

Score

an SFF symphony

An anthology with an emotional score from the heights of joy to the depths of despair – but always with a little hope shining through.

Reading 5X5

Five stories, five times

See how different writers take on the same material.

Reading 5X5

Writers' Edition

Two extra stories, the story seed, and authors' notes on writing.

Vestige

Novelettes, novellas, and novels by Metaphorosis authors.

The Nocturnals
Mariah Montoya

Night is Dangerous.
Day is deadly.

Where day and night last thirty years, humans move constantly stay ahead of the night and cruel Nocturnals that call it home. But a boy is lost out there.